I0550490

NEW BLOOD

Karl Anthony

This is a work of fiction. All rights reserved.
Copyright © 2012 Karl Anthony

No part of this book may be reproduced or transmitted in any form or by any means, electronic or mechanical, including photocopying, recording, or by any information storage and retrieval system, without permission in writing from the copyright owner.

ISBN 9780615665184 (paperback)
ISBN 9798777970947 (hardcover)

For more information, or to contact the author:

authoranthonypathfinder@gmail.com
www.anthonypathfinder.com

This book was printed in the United States of America

To those whose support has never wavered and insisted on me publishing this work, I thank you. Oly, I appreciate all that you have done.

EPISODE
1

The year was 1786. I had lived a despicable and horrid life up to that point. I was a slave on Kyle Buchanan's plantation. Called the Big House, life as I knew it on the plantation, was shattered forever as the wailing of the slaves and the Buchanan's reverberated throughout the night. The thing is, I wasn't worried about the Buchanan's. My only concern was my well-being and that of my family. My wife Evelyn and two girls were in the slave quarters waiting for me. I had left them to fetch water from the cistern pipe, near the old shed. It was against the rules for slaves to go outdoors at night. She was thirsty and I took the chance. I was confronted by Buchanan. He objected to my reasoning for being outside the slave quarters. He was angry and threatened to whip me. We had a heated exchange. Suddenly, there was a rustle, strange hissing sounds came from the old shed. There was a look of fear in Buchanan's eyes as he abruptly stopped talking in mid-sentence — turned and ran.

Taken aback, I fled in the direction of the slave quarters, only to be confronted by a tall handsome man with dark black eyes and chiseled features. His complexion was fairer than the Buchanan's. It was snow white. For a split second, I wasn't afraid; it wasn't as if I did it of my own free will. Something beckoned me. Within seconds, he viciously attacked me, and as his teeth sunk into my neck. Visions of my past life flashed in front of my eyes. I saw images of worlds long ago which were a mystery to me. I fought valiantly. But he was too powerful, and he quickly overpowered me.

As I glanced in his direction, standing beside him were two young women and a dark-haired young man. They hissed and opened their mouths wide enough for me to see their fangs, as they vanished in a blur in the direction of the slave quarters and the Big House. As I looked at the Big House from where I stood, my senses were heightened. I could taste, see, and feel everything that existed in my mind and thoughts. I was overcome with a voracious and insatiable hunger and thirst. It was beyond anything based on reason, as my every movement was increased at a phenomenal rate. I was paralyzed from fear as I wondered if my wife and daughters had met the same fate. I refused to venture to the slave quarters or Big House. I turned and walked away as the urge I felt compelled me.

I was terrified as I wandered around the Virginia woodland that forsaken night. I walked from one plantation to another, and I heard the terrifying screams and wails. I was befriended by a young couple, Isabel and Benjamin; they were the children of Alexander Monroe, a callous and brutal slave-owner. We all shared the same faith and were confused as we wandered on, unsure of what to do in the darkness — when the figure of a man appeared. He was with a group of men and women. I watched with fear as he introduced himself.

"I am Tazar, and this is my family," he said in an authoritative voice, as the others looked on.

"I am John," I barely managed to say. Benjamin and Isabel introduced themselves. I quickly realized that he was a friend of the man who attacked me.

"Come with us," he said in the same authoritative voice.

There wasn't any hesitation on our part. We followed him as he asked. He spoke continuously with the others, and I overheard one of them say, "We must return as soon as our task is complete." Tazar interrupted the one who spoke and abruptly let out a loud hiss. It was deafening to my ear. It was obvious he was a leader. Yet he was only an underling of Kovak, the one who turned me, I would later find out.

We were rescued by Tazar and his coven that night. Isabel and Benjamin would become my lifelong friends and confidantes. My hunger and thirst had reached epic proportions. Yet I was not one hundred percent. They led us to a group of terrified humans running for their lives.

"You are hungry, aren't you?" Tazar asked, waving his hands towards the group.

"We are," Benjamin replied as Isabel, and I nodded. At that moment, the only thing that mattered was quenching the thirst and hunger that filled my mind and thoughts.

KARL ANTHONY

"Well, there's your meal, eat and be merry," Tazar said, as he swooped down on the group of humans with the coven in pursuit. Isabel, Benjamin, and I followed closely behind. We moved at a rapid pace; unlike anything I had ever seen. The three of us could only look and wonder in amazement as the others flew above us. I was amazed by our acceleration as we kept pace with them. We pounced upon the humans. We ate greedily. I feasted on the blood of several terrified humans. The onslaught was over within minutes. Tazar signaled for us to follow, but I didn't respond. I had always been a free thinker despite my years as a slave.

"How dare you not follow?" a member in the group snarled, hissing.

"It's alright," Tazar smiled. "He was captured and forced to do for others as they did to our kind before, we were turned. Let him have his moment. He will come around."

The coven turned and flew to the skies with Isabel and Benjamin behind on foot. I had to make a split-second decision. I could still see and hear them, but things were quickly fading. I couldn't return to the Big House. I couldn't go and live with humans. I was no longer one of them. I was one of the undead and I needed to know why I was turned. Why wasn't I destroyed like the humans we attacked? I had questions that needed to be answered, and as their smell and scent began to fade, I followed in pursuit.

***

4

I couldn't fathom everything that had taken place in such a brief time in my life. I was enslaved at the age of twenty, and I was only twenty-seven years old when I was turned. Before these chains of events, I was a freeman. I had studied in many of the great educational centers of the world. The news came that the thirteen colonies that were under British rule had gained their independence. I and a few of my mates, after the Treaty of Paris in 1783 verified the independence, decided to travel to America. I was from an established family as were my mates. I was to study in America along with several of my seafaring mates. However, upon entry, I was abducted and sold into slavery. My mates pleaded with my capturers that I was a freeman and that I was born on the coast of Africa to a privileged family and that I was a seaman. They erupted in laughter. My mates were lucky to leave alive. They were released and given passage to sail wherever they pleased as long as it wasn't on the shores of America. I was taken by force to the slave auction block and sold to the Buchanan. Standing six-three with handsome features, I was in perfect physical shape.

In the early stages of my enslavement, I worked primarily as a house servant. I also did odd jobs in and around the house. I did this until I became Mrs. Buchanan's official carriage driver. She took a likening to me. I trusted her and I revealed to her that the rumors she heard about me knowing how to read and write were true.

Mr. Buchanan heard the stories but didn't believe them until his wife told him they were true. He was angry. There were whispers of me being sold to one of his close friends, who lived in North Carolina, and the buyer would arrive soon to get me.

KARL ANTHONY

He felt the fear of being sold would do me some good, as far as keeping me in my place. I never liked him. I did everything possible to avoid a confrontation with him. He would stare at me with icy cold eyes, especially when someone was getting whipped. It was Mrs. Buchanan who spoke on my behalf and saved me on numerous occasions. He wanted to teach me a lesson and he eventually did, by putting me to work in the fields, quite different from my carriage driving duties.

EPISODE 2

It wasn't long before we approached a sprawling mansion in the remote town of Leicester, Massachusetts. Hidden by countless dirt roads and several foundations, including a collapsed barn and lots of stone walls, the mansion blended in perfectly with the other immense houses. Yet, I couldn't fathom how far and how quickly we traveled.

My sense of direction and judgment was no longer important. And as we approached the front door, Tazar moving swiftly opened it and motioned for us to enter. As a slave, I was forbidden to enter the house through the front door. It was customary for slaves that worked in the fields to enter through the back door, and only when told to do so.

I was hesitant, and as Isabel and Benjamin entered ahead of me, they turned and looked at me, as if to say, what is he doing? Tazar had

7

a slight smile on his face and as he and the coven members ushered me in, I trembled with fear. Tazar put a hand on my shoulder. A cold shudder traveled through my body unlike anything, I had felt before.

"Don't be alarmed, it's okay," he said, reassuringly as we headed into a huge study, the likes of which I had never seen before.

"Thank you, sir."

"There's no need for that," he smiled.

I could hear the voices and thoughts of those inside the house albeit in a rambling, garbled, and unclear drawl, lacking coherence. The transformation from human to one of the undead hadn't fully reached its capacity, because I was unable to understand what they were saying. Thus, it sounded confusing and jumbled. However, there was a powerful force emanating from a great presence inside the house. There was a commanding aura to it, and it exuded fear, respect, and admiration. It was more powerful than what I felt when I first saw, Tazar. I was speechless and looked on with incredulous disbelief as the face of Kovak, my maker appeared. There was a beautiful girl with him. Tana was her name, and she was his most trusted assistant. Kovak was imposing and charming. There was a pleasant look on his face.

"Welcome to our world," he said, extending his hands outwards. Several unimaginable thoughts ran through my mind. "Don't be afraid, John Buchanan. You are amongst friends. Speak."

"What happened to me? How do you know my name? Why me? I'm only a . . ."

"No," he said cutting me off, in that same well-mannered voice of his. "You are not a slave or were you meant to be one of those were the words you were about to say. This is your destiny. As I said before, John Buchanan, you are with friends."

I was about to tell him that I was a simple man. I never considered or referred to myself as a slave, never. I think he knew what I was going to say, but for whatever reason, he chose to say that.

"What about my family? My wife and children, where are they?"

"I do not know of whom you speak." There was an uncanny silence as he slowly turned his head to the side and looked at Isabel and Benjamin, before turning his attention to Tazar.

"What is it that you need to know?" Tazar said to him.

"Ah, it was you who brought these two amongst us, huh, Tazar?"

"Indeed."

"And what should I call them?"

"Give him your names," he said to them, as the coven of more than thirty vampires looked on.

"I am called Benjamin Monroe, and this is my sister . . ."

Cutting him off, Kovak said, "Ah, your name most beautiful one, is?"

"Isabel," she uttered in an almost childlike voice, a far cry from the talkative daughter of Alexander Monroe. My master would stop by their plantation to trade barbs about their respective slaves. And on those occasions, I would see her, Benjamin, and their other siblings.

"Wonderful! Isabel, you are such a beauty."

There were whispers coming from a buxom blonde and a raven-hair girl, whose features mirrored each other. I later found out they were identical twins, and the blonde was Kovak's eternal lover, Savina. She and her sister, Ravina, have been with Kovak for over two thousand years. There was also a handsome young man, who appeared to be no older than twenty-five standing next to Ravina. His name was, Koshen. He stared at me with wary eyes. Kovak turned and looked at the girls with raised eyebrows. They immediately lowered their heads.

"Kovak, are you done with them?" Tazar asked.

"Yes. Hold on. John Buchanan, from this day forward you will be called, Salas."

Kovak then turned and walked away with Tana by his side. A group of twelve men and women followed closely behind. They were known as the Council and the Argi. Their duties required them to uphold the bylaws of the coven and to pass judgment and make decisions based solely on the actions of those who would dare to violate the coven's decree.

The Argi was also the last intermediary between the Council and those who violated the coven's decree. Nonetheless, Kovak's words were final. Not only was he the leader of his coven, but he was the master of several others. The leaders of these covens paid homage to him and if they refused, they were immediately destroyed.

As the months and years passed, the thoughts I had of returning to the Big House were nothing but a memory. Everything that I had been or ever wanted in life up to that point, died inside me that fateful night. I knew I would never return to the place where I lost my beloved and children. It had become an unknown place to me. Surely, I had thoughts of walking away from the coven, but would they allow it? I asked myself.

***

I decided to venture into town one night, unsure of myself and what to do. There, I met a young woman. She reminded me of my beloved. Her beautiful brown eyes and flawless skin immediately overwhelmed my senses. I was uneasy and nervous as she watched me from a distance. I was petrified that she may have figured me out. I fled, but she followed closely behind. The hunger that raged in me needed to be fed and I thought she would be a great meal.

Instead, I was in for more than I could chew as she attacked me. Her strength was beyond anything I could ever imagine, but within seconds, I had overpowered her. With my body pressed against hers, she told me that she followed me only because she knew that I was one of the undead and that I was a newborn. Nonetheless, she smiled and said her main reason was that she found me handsome.

Her flesh felt soft against mine and although Evelyn was still fresh in my memory, the fire and desire that raged inside me needed to be quenched. She took me on a sexual bliss that I had never experienced even as a human. My manhood seemed to grow in length inside her, the more she rode me. Her secret garden drove me wild.

Her eyes penetrated me and the depths of it magnified my intensity and emotions. Our eyes mirrored each other as our hisses and moans pushed us to another stratosphere as I sunk myself deeper inside her. It was a bond of lust that we shared at that moment.

"Fuck me, harder!" she whispered in my ear. "I have never fucked a vampire like you."

"And I have never fucked a woman like you."

"What is your name?"

"Salas," I managed to utter.

"I am Febra. I am from the Dalical coven." I didn't know what to say. I had no idea of my coven's name. "Come with me and my coven."

"I can't do that."

"Why not?"

"I just can't."

"I can protect you."

She kissed me passionately. All our senses were heightened as our lovemaking deepened. She rode me steadily as I held onto her and stroked her faster and harder. We ravished each other bodies as we hissed and exploded together.

"I have to go now," I said.

"Give it a chance, come with me."

I explained to her that I couldn't do such a thing. She said she understood, but that if I changed my mind that I was welcome. She then gave me a deep kiss before taking off in a blur. It was an amazing night, to say the least. It was a sexual interlude that I will never forget. Over the years, whenever our desire for each other raged, we found a way to quench it. Our secret rendezvous was known only to us.

EPISODE

3

Both Kovak and Tazar treated me well. Our raids on the unsuspecting humans created an environment that saw some of our coven members destroyed by the humans and members of the warring vampire coven, the Xeras. They were led by the vicious and cold-blooded, Lazan. He was battle-tested according to Tazar. He along with Tazar and Kovak were once close. They were turned by the same vampire.

It was a time when our kind was unknown to humans, and we lived amongst them without fear or suspicion. We fed on them freely. They believed it was the work of wild animals and the roaming vagabonds that were responsible for these horrible acts. The darkness was our ally and Lazan and Trajar along with Kovak and Tazar were inseparable as they savagely fed on the humans.

KARL ANTHONY

Despite their close friendship, Lazan and Trajar began plotting against Kovak and Tazar, because of their closeness with their maker. Together, they devised a plan that would forever change their relationship. Trajar befriended a down-on-his-luck human and through fear and manipulation; he convinced him to participate in his and Lazan's diabolical plan.

They had him remove their coffins to an unknown location. And as the others slept, the scared human returned and open the windows and coffins, as he was told. With the sun at its peak, the doomed vampires were burned to eternal damnation. More than half of the coven met their fate on that hot sunny day. The sun was our enemy in those days. Kovak, Tazar, their maker, and several vampires made it out alive.

When confronted by the others concerning their whereabouts, Lazan and Trajar lied and blamed it on the humans. Believing them, the coven attacked and killed as many humans as they could the following night.

Trajar and Lazan's accomplice was the first fatality as they both attacked him, ripping him apart. Tazar said he had always suspected both Lazan and Trajar, but he didn't have enough proof. It pained their maker, he said, because he thought so highly of the two and whenever the issue was brought up, he would only sigh and ask them not to talk about it.

This was only the beginning of a few violations and rules which Lazan and Trajar would violate. These were rules that the Argi, the Council, and our ancestors had followed for thousands of years. According to Tazar, there were three established covens of vampires that were the dominant group in the Old Country. The other covens were splintered groups of mercenary fighters who were motivated solely by the desire of hunting and drinking human blood, and the yearning to join one of the dominant covens.

What Lazan and Trajar did was beyond anyone's imagination. They invited the Priesthood of the early Christians into our sanctuary and shared many of our most treasured secrets. They somehow convinced the Priesthood that we needed salvation from our eternal walk, that we needed it from their god, and that we longed for this salvation.

The Priesthood believed this deception and would visit our sanctuary at night. We thought about ripping their heads from their bodies, Tazar said, but our maker and the other elders were worried about an all-out assault on our kind by the humans. The Priesthood knew we were nightwalkers, and they came prepared, they brought with them several weapons and waters that were anointed by their god to keep us from damnation, but at the same time could destroy us.

Their scent smelled of death, and when we rejected their offers and drove them from our midst, they used their oils, water, and other ointments in our place of sleep. They weren't aware of it, Tazar said until their numbers began dwindling.

Lazan and Trajar permitted and allowed them into our midst, while we slept. Humans were forbidden into our sleeping chambers, Tazar continued. This was the law and they violated it, and years later they would do it again, he ended.

"Why didn't the elders destroy them?" I asked.

"There were some in the rank and file, who believed that we could live as humans do."

"This was outrageous thinking, Tazar."

"Indeed, my son. Some members of the Argi and the Council supported these two fools. The warring factions against us were more intense than it is now, Salas. We had the humans on one side and some of our kind on the other, and they were determined in trying to appease the humans, thus the constant battles."

"Why didn't you take out Lazan and Trajar?"

"Indeed, I understand you clearly, but in those days, things were done differently. I was a young vampire then, and when the Argi spoke, you had to do as told. I tell you this because I want you to know that eventually you will be faced with some of these problems, if not now, then it will be years later, but it will happen."

"I understand, Tazar. What happened to the three dominant covens?"

"We were at war amongst ourselves and eventually disbanded and became splintered and fragmented like the others. It was only because of me and Kovak's resolve that we were able to do what we did. And I refused to let anyone destroy what he and I have worked so hard to put together. I love who and what we are my son. We are the undead. We have a glorious past, and there are those amongst us, our kind that thinks like humans and would love to see our destruction."

I listened intently to his every word. I soaked it all up. Tazar's words filled me and gave me a renewed spirit. I would give my life for him, Kovak, and the coven.

***

I wanted to hear more. I was captivated by the stories and the very next day I sat down with Tazar once again. He began by saying that their maker was deeply anti-religious and untrustworthy of those who weren't. Their maker carried a sword on his side and drank from a crystal bottle of the finest blood. According to Tazar, Kovak modeled himself after their maker. It was sometime after the Crusade that their maker was captured by the Christians and destroyed. Forced to flee, because of the fervor and antagonistic behavior of the humans, the covens went underground. Disappeared! Vanish, as if they never existed.

During this period of isolation, an incredible transmutation took place when the covens reappeared. The metamorphosis of their bodies and cells allowed the covens to move around freely in the daylight. This transmutation gave our kind, a new lease on life. It was a new beginning for the covens. Unlike anything they had confronted before as their sworn nemesis, the sun was no longer a threat. Their new rebirth saw them walking in the daylight and living amongst the humans while maintaining their duality as the undead.

This was a new beginning for all the vampire covens throughout the Old World. Yet there was a price that some would have to pay. The fervor from the Christian-Judeo beliefs and propaganda still abound. The numbers of casualties were high, as humans and vampires alike were burned at the stake. If one were suspected of heresy and other innate intellectual curiosities deemed offensive to the Church and charged with any of those offenses one would be burned at the stake. Kovak and Lazan's maker was caught in the twisted fervor.

KARL ANTHONY

Not known for his logic or reasoning, Lazan blamed Kovak for the abrupt death of their maker. His was one of the oldest of all the covens that existed, the Vladzann. However, what Lazan failed to take into consideration was that their maker mingled freely amongst the humans, who had their suspicion about him. He had also made several comments questioning the legitimacy of the human god, after losing his temper.

Unbeknownst to him, several of them were skilled vampire hunters and knew the ways of the undead. They plotted his destruction and trapped him. He fought valiantly, killing as many of them as he could; but they were prepared, and he was captured and burned at the stake. Lazan believed that Kovak and Tazar's lovers witnessed the capture of their maker, but said nothing about it, fearing reprisal.

With revenge on his mind, Lazan destroyed Kovak and Tazar's beloved, and others of our coven. He fled deeper into the Old country with Trajar, and as they tracked them from Romania to Hungary and across other lands, unfortunately, they lost their scent and that of their coven. For years, they heard nothing of their whereabouts. It wasn't until the Spaniards decided to trek to the North American continent that Kovak learned that they had traveled and settled into what is now, Virginia — my old home.

I was more than willing to hear what else Tazar had to say about the origins and historical background of my maker. I was now one of the undead and knowing this was important. It was who I am. As a slave, I belonged to the Buchanan's, but in a vastly different way from my coven. Here, I belonged.

I could have fled the coven-like others had done in the past if I thought I did not belong. But would it have made sense? Would being on my own be a better solution? That was a question I never wanted to answer.

I was berated at times as I tried to adapt to my new existence. I was teased and ridiculed at times, but I took it all in stride. I wanted to learn about this world, for what it was, and what it had become. I needed to understand its meanings and pitfalls. My thoughts remained focused on soaking up everything that would help me in understanding my shortcomings along this unknown path. I yearned for that mental reasoning that would explain the rationale for my present situation. I craved it, and the one person that could accommodate it at that moment was, Tazar. At least, it would satisfy my rambling thoughts until I found that place within myself that I was looking for.

Kovak and Tazar led a significant coven of vampires in pursuit of Lazan, he continued. They finally collared him and destroyed him and a few of his fighters, after three days of a fierce battle in the Callahans hills of Virginia. Trajar, who was Lazan's second in command first fled to Connecticut and later settled in Massachusetts.

"With Lazan's death, did the fighting end?" I asked.

"No, it hasn't, and I don't think it ever will. Kovak has sworn that he will rid the underworld of Lazan's memory. And he will do likewise to Trajar and his coven of vampires. Are you worried?"

"Should I?"

"No, not at all, you seem capable enough of handling yourself."

"I see."

"Lazan's fighters are vicious, more so than us. We only retaliated because we had no other choice. They seek to destroy all the other vampire covens and rule by themselves. Trajar is just as vicious as

Lazan was, if not worse. We are not the warring type. We would rather live alongside humans and feed on them without them knowing. But Trajar, no, he wants the humans to know. He wants them to fear him, which they already do. Yet the humans do not see us differently, one from the other. In their eyes, we are all murderous cold-blooded killers. And it is this that Trajar has lost sight of."

"So, you thought that after Lazan's demise, he would be more compromising and make peace?"

"Surely, we did. Kovak tried his best to persuade him to join our ranks as brothers once again. He accepted but was only being pretentious. He befriended a group of humans who were anxious to destroy our kind, and he obliged them by allowing them to murder over twenty of our brothers and sisters."

"Just like he did in the past, huh?"

"Indeed, Salas. There would and could never be any reconciliation after that vicious attack."

"What became of the humans?"

"You were a part of it. You saw the outcome."

"This is recent?"

"Yes, and Mr. Buchanan was one of the human ringleaders."

No wonder he panicked like he did that night when he accosted me. He knew. I thought to myself.

EPISODE
4

Time wasn't kind to the humans who faced their mortality, as well as the blood-thirsty vampire covens that preyed on them. I was awestruck as I watched the humans grow old. The same fate met my friends from my days on the plantation. Human death was something that I thought I would have experienced. Although death wasn't something that I thought about in my younger days, nonetheless, the very minute that I was captured and sold like an animal; I yearned for the day when I would face my maker.

Like everyone else, longevity was something I had hoped for, but I never imagined it would come this way. And as I looked at my physical appearance and ran my fingers over my face, I still had the smooth young skin and youthful looks of my twenty-seven years. I couldn't say the same for those humans who were wrinkled and aged. Were they better off than me, because I never had the opportunity to grow old and experienced what it was like? I shuddered to think that it was only me, who felt this way. Is death as a human a condemnation, or me being one of the undead is? I pondered these things as I would observe the humans who were unaware that I was one of the undead.

Never in a million years did I expect anything like this, as I outlived the humans and adapted to their ever-creative and inventive means by which they lived. Humans were changing the world around us, and we had to adapt to their changes. At times, I would foolishly think that I was still human. I lived and walked alongside them. Yet as quickly as I had those thoughts, I quickly dismissed them.

I was reminded of what some of the older vampires described as the glory days. They said as the years passed, and the ongoing battles between our coven and Trajar's continued, both covens were ecstatic when the humans revolted against each other and fired the first shot, signaling the start of the Revolutionary War.

Our coven welcomed the fighting with open arms. Reveling and enjoying every moment of it. They feasted on the soldiers gleefully. Trajar's coven was a part of the vicious attacks. A handful of fragmented covens who wanted no part of either coven joined the feast. It was a celebration, Salas, you should have been there, they ended, salivating from their mouths.

***

A hundred years had passed, and I still hadn't forgotten about my one true love, Evelyn. My heart ached constantly. I recalled her kissing me on the lips and telling me to be careful that fateful night. The recurring nightmares of her and my children were taking a toll on me. I would awake from my sleep craving her warmth. I didn't know if this was normal behavior for a vampire. What I did know is that I didn't give a damn. Whilst everyone was preoccupied and seemed content with their relationships, there was a burning desire within my loins that craved Ravina. Koshen watched my every move whenever she and I spoke.

I knew that he desired her. Still, I never got the impression that she felt the same. His icy cold stares would have made an ordinary vampire quake in his boots, but no, not me. Surely, I was aware that he was turned before me. Even so, I never allowed it to become an issue. I was prepared. My thoughts and my body were on a collision course that would have eventually led to my eternal demise. Noticing my wayward ways, Kovak and I would spend many nights talking.

"I know your pain. I understand. There was a time when I felt as you did. It took me a while to gather myself. Tell me about this, Evelyn?" Kovak asked me one night.

As I reminisced, I couldn't help smiling, "She was tall and beautiful with soft brown eyes and smooth brown skin. It was flawless. She was something to behold. From the moment that I laid eyes on her; I knew she would be mine. All the men in the slave quarters desired her, but she chose me, Kovak." Kovak smiled, as I continued. "Only one other man slept with her before I did, and that was my master. And after she became my wife, he would call her to the Big House. It hurt me a lot. I thought about taking his life, but I feared reprisal, not so much for myself, but for her."

"Ah, men of his kind were not worthy to be called, Men. I see that you are passionate about your lost love, and I have something that I must share with you."

"You do?"

"Yes, our coven is one of the oldest in vampiredom. My maker was a great vampire. He taught me everything about our origins and coven. It is many of these things that I have shared with you since you have been with us. I only provide and share this kind of information with those that I consider worthwhile amongst us. I know that Tazar shared some things with you as well, so I won't bore you by repeating them. But I will say this, before continuing. The deception orchestrated by Lazan and Trajar put us at a disadvantage for many years. To deliberately mislead others by acts of tricks and treachery with the intent to harm our brothers and sisters is something that I am more aware of, and I want you to be my other eyes."

"Me?"

"Yes, my son!"

"It is a great honor, and I will."

Nodding his head, he continued, "The Argi and I discussed these concerns and we all agreed that you, Salas, should know these things."

He told me the history of his coven and maker and briefed me on where I fit in. He made it known to me that I wasn't just an ordinary vampire, but one with a purpose within the coven. He had chosen me to be a part of the rank and file and a close acquaintance. I was overwhelmed and humbled to be regarded in such high esteem alongside Tazar and the others.

"I'm entrusting you with a lot of responsibilities and I know you will not let me down."

"You have made a wise choice. I will not let you down. I won't let anything stand in our way. Our coven will reign supreme above all."

"Ah, wonderful, our survival rests upon all our shoulders, our nemesis is well prepared, so we have to be more than ready at all times."

"Hmm," I said, agreeing.

"There's something else that I want to share with you concerning your beloved, Evelyn." My eyes widened as my anticipation heightened. "Did Tazar tell you that Mr. Buchanan was known to us?"

"Yes, he did."

"He was among a group of humans whose ancestors have hunted us since our arrival here on the North American continent. He was one of the leaders of the group that destroyed several members of our coven. That night by the barn wasn't a coincidence at all. We watched you night after night as you fetch water for your family. So, we waited for Mr. Buchanan to show up, and he did. We were surprised that he wasn't properly armed to defend himself against us. Yet the weaponry he had could have easily killed another human, and that night he came intending to take your life. He never expected to see us, or he would have been much better prepared. If you recalled, right before I appeared to you, he ran. When I got inside the house your children were already dead. He had murdered them."

I cried out. I was still for a moment as I composed myself. "What about, Evelyn?"

KARL ANTHONY

"I didn't see her until later. Bodies were lying around. Mr. Buchanan had murdered his family. I heard the screaming of a woman. But I was distracted by the smell of the servants of the household. When I got done and made my way to where the screams were coming from, Mr. Buchanan had destroyed four of our members. With blinding speed, I tore into his flesh, deliberately making sure that he would join me in eternal damnation and where I would take my full revenge. I also wanted him to live as one of the undead and see what it's like.

Your beloved Evelyn was wounded and lying in a corner of the family room, calling your name. I knew it was you. So, I granted her wish, which was to see you. But during the fracas, another group of humans intervened, and my coven and I fled. I left her behind. I don't know what became of her.

I have tried to summon her on numerous occasions and there hasn't been any response. I did the same with Mr. Buchanan and it was the same result. Over the years, I have second-guessed myself as to whether I turned either of them. Lately, I have had my doubts. The humans played a role in it, and if so, I'm sorry for your grief and pain."

"I'm grateful, Kovak. You gave me something that I had been missing all these years."

"And what is that?"

"Closure! Now, I can have some peace of mind, knowing that she asked for me. She was thinking about me. Yes, she was." As our conversation ended, he told me that we had some unfinished business. He had gotten some information on Trajar's whereabouts.

EPISODE

5

Days later . . .

The place we chose to ambush Trajar, and his coven was treacherous and unsafe land. As we approached, their scent overwhelmed us. The sound of cracking tree branches and the shuffling of feet could be heard in the distance. My senses were heightened as the noise became louder. Kovak, Tazar, and Ravina took to the skies leaving me, Koshen, and Savina in command of the ground troops. Benjamin and Isabel stood next to me as our hisses slowly began echoing and our fangs protrude.

Within seconds, our hisses were returned by our adversaries as we crouched slightly, ready for attack. The assault began. I ripped two of Trajar's warrior's heads off. Benjamin and I soared into a group of our enemies with the others close behind. I looked skyward. I caught a glimpse of Kovak and Trajar battling each other. Tazar was doing the same with Trajar's second in command. Ravina was busy grappling with two young female fighters. They were strong and vicious.

I was up against a young, but powerful vampire. With blinding speed, I ripped his face into tiny shreds of blood-splattered strips. He was reeling from the vicious attack, and with blood oozing from his wounds, he crumbled to the ground. His face was darkened with pain as he squirmed uncontrollably. There was a look of horror on his face as his gaze darted back and forth as if he was looking for help. He had accepted his faith and as he lay in the fetal position and about to make the transition into eternal paradise, I swooped in and viciously ripped his neck from his body.

Koshen severed the head of two of our adversaries. He then flew into a small group that viciously attacked him. He held his own as he fought fearlessly. I swooped down and unleashed a brutal assault upon the group. We slaughtered them with sheer thrill, as the snapping and breaking of body parts and blood flew all around us. We acknowledged each other and flew into another group that fought us ferociously. In no time, we had wiped them out, as blood streaked from our mouths and hands. I glanced at him, and he smiled. His approach and his fighting skills were quite impressive.

"Well done, Salas!" he said.

"We are here to defend and protect our coven from the likes of those who wish to destroy us," I stated, and he nodded his head in agreement.

"Come, let us go and help the others."

"Indeed, I'm with you."

At times, my vision was blurred by the enormous amount of blood that flew. It was a remarkable sight as the carnage and blood spewed and soaked the ground, turning it into a crimson red color. We had them on the run. They were no match for us. We were getting the better of them as they took to the skies. We were in pursuit before Kovak called us off. Once again, Trajar had gotten away, but this time he was injured. There were casualties on both sides, and they feared far worse than ours. We gathered the bodies at once and lit them.

"Why did you let him get away? Why didn't you let us stay on their tails?" I said to Kovak.

"Ah, I should have, right? But he was a bit elusive and even though he's injured, we don't know what kind of trap he may have set for us," Kovak, grimaced.

The coven took to the skies and disappeared into the cool Massachusetts night.

***

Several things had unfolded with my new family. Kovak began an affair with Isabel. And although he and Savina remained lovers, the tension was unbearable. Savina, aware of their affair could do nothing about it. She instead took her frustration out on Isabel whenever the opportunity presented itself.

Aware of her mistreatment of Isabel, Kovak warned her on several occasions. Not one to take heed to a threat, especially from Kovak, someone whom she has been with for many years was mind-boggling. She was dealt with harshly. However, I for one never felt sorry for her. I knew her pedigree and type.

KARL ANTHONY

A few of the vampires were smitten by Isabel's beauty and physical assets as was I, but I knew she was off-limits. I came to that conclusion the night we were brought to the mansion. Despite being turned the very same night as I was, Isabel was at times naive, and it would be on full display in the coming years.

I was convinced early on that Ravina was attracted to me. From the outset, she pretended as if she wasn't, but I knew better. She had listened to my conversations with Kovak and Tazar and she knew that I was highly regarded by the Council. It was one thing to pretend as if I wasn't aware, which I never did. Yet I was worried about Koshen. His attitude and demeanor had lessened recently. Still, he couldn't bear seeing me and Ravina together, no matter how insignificant the reasons were.

Kovak made it clear to me that she was smitten with my elegance, eloquence, and charm. For someone who had only a short time ago become one of the undead, everything that I did with the coven and my fiercest warrior-like swagger in battle, appealed to her and she respected that. Aware of this, I offered her a night out and a carriage ride in the bustling town of Boston.

All eyes were on us as she held my arm in the manner a lady ought to, and as we walked down the avenue, the stares from the many onlookers were unbearable. They were aghast at seeing a black man with a white woman on his arm.

Unbeknownst to them, we weren't an ordinary couple. Ravina and I returned their intense stares with cold chilling glares of our own. Even the carriage driver seemed to have had a problem with us until I handed him enough money that would last him for at least three days. His response was an uneasy smile. He held Ravina's hand as she got into the carriage, and I saw the horrified look on his face when he felt the coldness of her hand. I supposed he would have run, but the fear he felt prevented him from doing so.

"Where are we going?" she asked in a seductive voice.

"Wherever destiny leads us," I replied.

"I didn't mean that."

"What then did you mean?" I smiled, knowing quite well what she meant. "Driver, give us the full tour." He reacted with some apprehension before doing as told. "So, my dear, isn't it a lovely night for us to be out?"

"I'd rather not say."

"And why is that?"

Suddenly, our moment together was interrupted by an angry outburst of, "Get the nigger! Get the nigger!" and shouts of "Why any decent white woman would be riding with a nigger?!" I turned and glanced at Ravina, who tried to explain to the small mob that it had grown into that I was only escorting her to her father's house, a well-established diplomat.

"Liars!" the carriage driver yelled, jumping from his seat. "They are lovers!"

There was a small group of soldiers stationed on the corner, who heard the commotion and decided to see what was going on.

"What is going on here?" one of the soldiers asked.

"That finely dressed nigger is with that white woman," an overweight woman with tattered clothes yelled. I was being patient, hoping that Ravina's idea might work.

"Is this true, madam?" the soldier asked her.

"Yes, it is," she answered, there was a loud groan from the crowd.

"Get them! Get the nigger!" the overweight lady screamed, urging the crowd on.

The mob didn't know what awaited them as Ravina with a burst of speed ripped the overweight lady's head from her body. With lightning speed, I mutilated the soldiers in a blur before they could fire a shot. And as the small mob dispersed and ran for their lives, I approached the carriage driver. He was pale as a ghost, and from his looks, he acted as if he had seen one; only thing was, I wasn't. I was a vampire. I ripped him apart, snapping his neck.

As we made our way back to the mansion, we knew it wouldn't take long for the mob to alert the other towns. Thus, preparing our sworn enemies the vampire slayers to come and hunt us down. This was the typical practice amongst humans. They lived for these moments.

In other words, we are the evil that their churches and holy books speak about. Yet I nor Ravina and others who must now live as one of the undead were as evil as humans. What about the humans who kidnapped me and sold me into slavery, weren't they evil? The humans who seek to destroy us, aren't they evil? So, I ask the question, who is good, and who is evil — and who or what gave them the right to decide if my kind is good or bad? These were some of the questions, I pondered.

Once we were back at the mansion, I told Kovak what happened. He smiled and softly said, "I believe they deserved what they had coming to them. I'll tell the others so they'll be mindful of the ignorant humans who will seek to take revenge."

EPISODE

6

That night, I ended up in Ravina's room. I felt awkward as if I were a virgin all over again. Other than Evelyn, Febra was the only other woman that I had been with. My mind was reeling back and forth, and I felt all sorts of emotions. Seeing my discomfort, Ravina who was standing across the other side of the room was suddenly in front of me. Her head rose to meet my lips and as I lowered mine, our lips touched. My thoughts seemed to explode within me, driving me to unknown depths that I had never encountered or felt before, not even with Febra.

As our kissing became more passionate, I couldn't control the thumping that I felt deep within my loins. She ran her tongue over my neck in an insatiable manner and deliberately began removing my clothes. I reciprocated as she shoved me onto the bed. I wasted no time as I began exploring her body and kissing her everywhere. She returned the favor with the same fire and desire, and when she straddled me; we became one as we drifted in and out of passion, clinging to one another.

As I lay there looking at her beautiful face and body, her rhythmic movements soon overwhelmed me, and in no time, I was moving at the same frantic pace. My mind was running wild. It was a passion-filled encounter that took control and weakened me. Her moans drove me crazy, and her protruding fangs grazed my neck, as she pinned my shoulders and rode me. My fangs were out and each time her mouth rubbed against my neck, I returned the favor, driving her into vampire ecstasy.

Our hands and kisses drove each other to the brink. I was swimming in her river of love and ecstasy. We were going at it for some time. Our bodies and minds were out of control. I envisioned and felt things that drove me over the edge, as we held each other and raced to the finish line. My inquisitiveness led me to want to know a lot more than what Kovak told me about her, as we lay there. She smiled as if she knew that I was going to ask her about her life.

"You knew, didn't you?"

"I didn't know exactly what it was that you were going to ask me. But I knew it was about me," she smiled.

Ravina's thoughts, senses, and smell were much older than mine. Like her and the others, I could hear the thoughts of humans easily. It wasn't the same amongst the undead, sure we can hear each other, but we cannot detect each other's thoughts. Only the wise ones share these unique gifts and that includes those who have been undead for ages, the Council, the Argi, Kovak, Tazar, Trajar, and others of his coven. I was merely a youngster compared to Ravina, but I was much older than her when she got turned. She was a youthful twenty years of age.

"You know my story and how I was turned. Would it be too much for me to ask you how you became one of the undead?"

"My sister and I were born on the island of Sicily, many years ago. We were happy young girls. We would help mother with the garden, where she grew vegetables to be sold in the town's market. My father was a carpenter. He had a small workplace, a few feet from our small but humble home.

One scorching summer evening, my father and some of his friends were drinking in one of the town's public houses, when a fight broke out. My father was beaten to death. When we got news of his death, my mother hurriedly left with us following behind her. We didn't live too far from the public houses.

When we got there a small group had gathered. My father's body was taken to our home. My mother was hysterical by now and wanted to know who did this to her husband. To our amazement, she was taken a few feet from the public house where five ravaged and bloody bodies laid. It was the most horrible thing I had ever seen when suddenly, Kovak and Tazar appeared. They seemed nice and the town accepted them, believing they were the ones who chased off the animals that had torn the men apart."

"Hmm, then what happened?"

"My mother invited them to our home. They would visit now and then. Savina and I were nineteen soon to be twenty. We were in love with one of the lord's sons and his cousin, but we were poor. It didn't stop them from pretending to stop by our home for other reasons if only to see us. This went on until our twentieth birthday. The night had caught us being escorted home by the boys and their driver. When suddenly, Kovak, whom we hadn't seen in a long time appeared, to our horror he attacked the three and ripped them apart. Frightened, we screamed, but it seemed as if nothing came out of our mouths. He moved in a blur and within seconds, we were in some unknown area. 'You have nothing to be afraid of,' he smiled. 'Come!' As if in a trance, we did as he said, and that's where he bit us both."

"You never asked him, why he did this to you and your sister?"

"Yes, I did. I knew he was in love with my sister. He had made it known to my mother."

"So why did he bite you?"

"He wanted us to be together."

"Did you ever get angry at him for doing this to you?"

"Yes, because I lost my mother and my family. I watched her die a human death and I couldn't do anything to prevent it. I thought about making her one of the undead. But Savina was against it. So, we let her live her life as the other humans did and enter their eternity. Over the years, those emotions have left my thoughts."

"I understand. I think everything happens for a reason. I have come to accept that now. Here I am with you and neither of us knew this moment would take place . . ."

Before I could finish my thoughts, she said, "Your Evelyn, do you still love her? And do you think you will ever see her again?"

I was taken aback by that question as I searched to find the right words to say.

"You know how I feel about her," I replied. We had only moments ago shared something wonderful. "Will, I ever see her again? That's a question that I will never be able to answer. What I do want you to know is that I love you and my eternity without you would be a thousand times more painful than what I felt as a human. What we have now is something that I don't ever want to change."

"I feel the same. But what if she surfaces? You and I have been around for so many years and have seen so many things. So why isn't it possible that perhaps one day she might show up?"

"Kovak has reached out to her for all those years, and nothing. I've done the same. And although my thoughts are not as powerful as his, I tried. Don't you think if she was one of the undead, she would have responded to Kovak? He's her maker. Look how long it's been? So then, isn't it fair to say that she's not one of the undead?"

"Very convincing my dear, what matters is you and I have each other now."

"And we always will."

"Oh, why haven't you told Kovak your true name?"

"It never occurred to me to do so."

"And why not? I think Karang Mohale is such a beautiful name."

Laughing, I said, "You do, huh?"

"Yes, I do. I think you should."

"Knowing Kovak, he probably knows," I laughed.

"It's possible," she added, smiling.

I told her that I would eventually tell him. I held her hand and stared into her eyes and told her that I love her. Ironically enough, neither of us mentioned a word about, Koshen.

EPISODE

7

Ravina and I began spending a lot more time together, and as the whispers led by Koshen became more noticeable, I knew it would only be a matter of time before things would come to a climax. Koshen and his closest friends, a small group of four were furious. The group was made up of two females and two males. They were all turned in their late teens and early twenties. Kovak and the others didn't seem to care nor had a problem with it. It wasn't long before Koshen confronted Ravina wanting to know why we spend so much time together.

"It shouldn't be of any concern to you," she told him.

"Why should it not be? You weren't behaving like this until he showed up," he said in an angry voice.

"I'm not a child and I will not allow you to do this to me. This is none of your business and if you continue to harass me, I will have no choice but to bring it to Kovak's attention."

He let out a hearty laugh, before saying, "Kovak? He doesn't care about our relationship. He has too many important things to worry about much less our little squabble."

"First of all, you and I are not having a squabble and secondly, we are not in a relationship."

Infuriated, he fumed, "I refused to be looked upon as a fool. You will not disrespect me. I will deal with him on my terms."

Ravina made it known to me how he felt. I thought about it and decided to confront him. Without a doubt, it troubled me. I approached him the next day in the study. He was having a conversation with his friends.

"I understand that there are some things that you would like to share with me."

"I do," he snarled, displaying his fangs as his four cronies displayed theirs as well.

"Go on."

"Don't you ever disrespect me, underestimate me, or challenge me. Do not forget your place. You are new to this coven, and I will not allow you to steal the heart of my, beloved."

"Is that it?"

"Yes, it is."

"Hmm, I will not stoop to your boyish attitude and behavior in Kovak's home. I respect him too much. I will say this, when the time comes, I will be waiting for you. As for Ravina, she doesn't need a spoiled childish vampire like you to warm her heart."

Suddenly, he and one of his male underlings were in my face, hissing and staring at me with piercing eyes. When out of nowhere, Kovak appeared. His hiss drew the others and in a split second, he snatched two of them by the throat; as the other three cowered on the side.

"I have been listening. And any disagreement amongst us is a violation of this coven and what we stand for. Are we clear?" Kovak said in a commanding voice — with an angry look on his face. I was shaken. His presence jolted something deep within me.

"Yes," all five uttered.

"Ah, come with me, Salas," he said, putting an arm around my shoulders. I was still shaking as he and I walked into the library. "Ravina has told me everything, including your name."

"She did?" I stuttered.

Laughing, he said, "Yes, and I think it is great that she would want to spend eternity with you. She's like a daughter to me now because I chose to make her one of the undead. I know she told you the story."

"Yes, she did."

"Ah, wonderful! I know you're asking yourself, why it is that I admonished them and not you, aren't you?"

"Yes."

"You've been with us less time than some of the others and you have demonstrated not only your loyalty but your competence and your impeccable skills as a warrior; all traits that this coven needs. If there's any regret that I made as one of the undead, it was with, Koshen. He was unread, unpolished, and unrefined when I encountered him. My thirst had overwhelmed my vision and thoughts the night I made him one of the undead. So, you see; I expect nothing of him in situations as such. He's a fierce warrior like you. I admire that. He's a stalwart young man whose skills have brought us many victories. However, I will not tolerate any behavior of this sort from anyone including you that would create a problem and lead to other dire predicaments. Do I make myself clear?"

"Absolutely!"

"Wonderful," he smiled. "Come with me, I want to show you something."

***

We walked to another side of the mansion and ended up in a chamber, where Tazar and four members of the Council were talking. As we approached, they got up and greeted, Kovak.

"Sit," he said. "I wanted to show Salas the new direction that we are heading in. Let's have a drink."

There in front of us was a sizable crystal bottle filled with the richest and reddest blood-prepared for a King. The bottle was placed on a gold-plated tray with several small gold cups. A female Council member poured the red liquid into the cups and handed one each to us.

"Kovak, this looks to be some of the rarest of blood. Am I worthy to drink of this?" Bursting out in laughter, he said to me, "Repeat what you just said?" I did, only loud enough for the others to hear. They burst out in laughter as well.

"Drink, my son," Tazar said, chuckling. "It's only horses' blood."

"Huh?" They laughed aloud once again.

They put the cups to their mouths and drank. "Go ahead, drink!" Kovak said smiling, as I put the cup to my lips. The sweet taste immediately hit me. It flowed through my body refreshing my thoughts. It touched every part of my undead being and replenished all my senses, sending me into an intoxicating frenzy of pure delight.

"This is wonderful," I smiled as they began laughing once again.

"We are trying our best to minimize our taking of human lives to survive. There must be another way for us to feed our hunger. Their blood is the sweetest of all living things. Our forefathers knew this, but the time has come for us to change our ways. Humans are creating a lot of new inventions and means by which to destroy us. We do not wish to see our kind destroyed and extinct. Therefore, if we can find a way to feed our hunger other than destroying humans, then maybe they will leave us alone. What do you think, Salas, any suggestions?" Kovak asked.

"It makes a lot of sense," I said in agreement, "but how and where would we get the needed blood to survive?"

"Ah, Tazar, please inform him."

"We would get the blood from the buildings where the humans keep their dead. We would take the blood immediately after the bodies are placed there. But it must be warm. As you do know, we can't drink the blood of humans that have been dead for hours. Also, the soldiers are always fighting amongst themselves, and their bodies we can easily take our blood from."

"I couldn't agree with you more. That is a full proof plan, seems all the steps have been covered."

"Then let's drink some more of the horses' blood," Kovak laughed as we joined in. "Now come, there's one other thing I would like to share with you."

We walked to his private study. He retrieved two huge books from a secured area in the study and opened them.

"Have a seat." I did as told. "Take a look and tell me what you think."

I began skimming through the pages when he stopped me.

"What is it? Did I do something wrong?"

"Not at all! Do you know any of these languages?"

"It looks like a combination of Erythraean-Archaic Egyptian, Akkadian, Sumerian, Hurrian, Semitic, Anatolian, Hellenic, Celtic, Tocharian, Persian, Germanic, and Romanian."

"Ah, excellent! Excellent! Your studies as a human were beyond extraordinary. These are the languages our ancestors spoke. Only a few of us remain fluent speakers of these languages. I want you to promise me that you will never let our origin and ancestry fade away like dust in the wind. Tazar and I along with the Argi and the Council have been around for years. How we have survived is beyond even my imagination. Yet we have.

An astute mind such as yours does not come along very often and it reminds me of my days as a boy in the great libraries of Timbuktu and Alexandria. I have been around that long my son. Surely, as the sun rises every morning and the moon awaits her turn at night, my eternal paradise awaits me. Yet I'm inclined to give you access to these great works so that you can continue our legacy, and even though you may not acknowledge it now when you get as old as I am, you will see to it that someone else carries on the mantle for our kind. Promise me you will?"

I was at a loss for words as I stood in front of this man, my maker; a man that I was supposed to be angry at for making me one of the undead, and I wasn't. I was compelled and was accepting and more than prepared to take on such a task. He placed a hand on my shoulder as he stood above me. I looked up at him and said, "I promise. Nothing will stop or prevent me from doing what you have asked of me."

"Wonderful, my son! Just wonderful! You must not only read and study these languages, but they must become a part of you as well. Knowing these old languages will allow you to communicate with the elders of the Old World. There are still quite a few around. It will allow you to learn and know the secrets of whence we came. I chose you because you are smart and intelligent, my son."

"But why, me?"

He smiled and then said, "Sometimes we are called to take up the mantle for the survival of others. It is called destiny, my son. It wasn't me who chose you. It chose you. Destiny chose you."

"I am humbled."

"Ah, don't worry, at least you're humbled. Me, I was scared when I was approached. I wasn't as humble as you are," he said, laughing. "Come, let's have a drink."

As I made my way back to my room, I had a lot on my mind. For hundreds of years, our kind had feasted on humans the only way we knew how. I had noticed for some time that our usual nightly rendezvous were becoming less frequent. Yet I never made much of it. We were being fed and that was all that mattered. I was glad the Council had confided in me and wanted to know how I felt.

Kovak was like a father to me, and I held that dear to my heart. He treated me like a son. He had put me in a position where my opinion mattered. I respected and admired him for that. The task ahead of us was a difficult one, but we were more than ready to see it through.

EPISODE

8

The early 1800s saw the country still a buzz from the formation of the New State and several of our closest allies also relished and held parties like the humans to commemorate the ongoing excitement of what took place in 1776. Unfortunately, I couldn't make it on time to escort Ravina to one of these festivities. Tazar and I along with a few others were making our depository from the town's morgues and elsewhere. When I finally arrived, I was taken aback by the splendor and opulence of the stately mansion. Several lion head gold statues adorned the entrance and plush crimson red carpet lined the walkway: leading up to a magnificent and regal-looking front door of the finest oak. A few lighted lamps illuminated the front of the mansion perfectly.

The affair was teeming with a plethora of covens, and they were all allies of ours. Tazar and I were immediately greeted by Kovak.

"Ah, you have arrived. How did things go?"

"It went well," Tazar assured him. I nodded in agreement.

"Gentlemen, if you will excuse me, I must go off and find, Ravina," I said.

"Certainly, go on. Tazar and I won't keep you any longer, will we?" Kovak remarked.

"Not at all, go on," Tazar added.

As I approached Ravina, I noticed she had a troubled look on her face.

"What is the matter?" I asked.

"It's Koshen. He's at it again."

"What did he do this time?" I turned around just in time as he was making his way around the room. And as I glared at him, he immediately stopped and smiled in my direction. "Continue," I said to Ravina.

She said they rode in Tazar's carriage to the ball. The mood was very subdued and quiet. Koshen initiated several conversations and was trying his best to convince her that I wasn't the right suitor; while trying not to be too confrontational, but at the same time trying to persuade her that he was a better suitor.

"I could tell he wanted me to go with him elsewhere. He pretended as if we were lost, which you and I both know is never the case. We arrived thirty minutes late and Kovak was furious at him."

"Hmm, he was, huh?"

"Yes, he was."

"What happened next?"

"Not much."

"Come, let's dance."

We were having quite the time as we enjoyed the festivities. Kovak who was a wonderful piano player began playing and asked me to join him. I did. A small crowd gathered, and I quickly noticed Koshen looking on with a smirk on his face.

After a few minutes of playing, I began to search the room to see where he was. I spotted him having a conversation with Benjamin in the adjoining room. I tried to probe his mind, but he blocked me from doing so. He smiled at me. Without any warning and with blinding speed, I confronted him. He was startled momentarily. I had never approached him in such a manner before.

"You stated how you felt the last time, now it's my turn. Leave her alone. I don't give a damn nor do I care how long ago you were turned. Stay the fuck away from her," I snarled as Benjamin looked on. I wasn't going to bring any additional attention to our little exchange, and it remained that way.

"You can't be serious, are you?" he asked with a creepy disturbing look in his eyes.

"Indeed, I am. And I will do everything in my powers to make sure that if you do overstep your boundaries, you will be dealt with accordingly."

Laughing, he said to Benjamin, "Do you know what he's talking about?" Benjamin didn't respond.

"I'm warning you this time and this time only. I will destroy you if you disrespect her. If you can't have a normal conversation with her, then you ought to not say anything to her. Do I make myself clear?"

"I'm scared. You're starting to sound more like Kovak. I don't give a fuck how friendly you are with him and your relationship with Ravina. I will rip your head from your limbs and send you to eternal damnation."

"We will see about that. We will see. Remember, I warned you," I said before turning and walking away. I was some distance away when I looked back to see what he was doing. His buddies were with him and from their smiles and demeanor; I guess he didn't tell them what happened. Benjamin approached me and wanted to know if I was okay. I told him I was fine.

"Are you sure? I can't stand his behavior either."

"I can't believe he still doesn't get it and would still try and pressure her about giving him a chance."

"Before you got here, he was being kind of aggressive. I told Isabel about it. She told Kovak, who glared at him, and he walked away from her."

"She told me. He is unbelievable. Why would you come to a gathering like this and behave like an idiot?"

"He has no class."

I laughed when Benjamin said that, coming from a slaveholding family, you would think if anyone didn't have any class it would be him and his family. Just the thought made me chuckle. Suddenly, I felt a slight breeze and Koshen was standing in front of me.

"What is this all about? You still don't get it, do you?"

"Damn you, Salas!" he snarled.

"No, not here! Salas, don't!" Benjamin cautioned me.

"You need to calm down," I said to Koshen. "Maybe some fresh air would do you good," I suggested to him.

"Fuck you! The time has come to put an end to this."

"Koshen, not here! I don't think you would want to embarrass Kovak with all his friends here," Benjamin warned him once again, and as he stormed off with a smirk on his face, he whispered in Savina's ear.

EPISODE

9

I didn't know what to make of the exchange between Koshen and Savina. The likelihood of the two — plotting against me, and Ravina was on my mind. I can understand their contempt towards me. I was elevated to a certain status within the coven by my esteemed ruler and King of the Vampires and maker, Kovak. I anticipated and expected their share of jealousy, but for Savina to plot against her sister troubled me deeply.

I was determined to find out if this was the case and as I stared into the darkness of the night from my bedroom window, I saw something move in the dark. With my suspicion aroused, I speedily approached it only to realize that it was a wild animal. When suddenly, I heard a rustle in the distance and instinctively reacted only to hear whatever it was run off into the night. My mind was racing back and forth. It was odd, to say the least. But I was in a reflective mood when I got back to my room. I watched the darkness give way to the sun and wondered if I would have accepted my faith so willingly if the sun was still our adversary.

***

What started as a somber morning only intensified no sooner than I entered the living quarters. I was approached by Tana, who informed me that Kovak needed my presence immediately. I thanked her and quickly made my way to the other side of the mansion. The area was off-limits to most of our coven brothers and sisters. Only a handful of us was allowed in this restricted area.

"I see that you received the message," Kovak greeted me alongside Tazar and Koshen. Surprised? Certainly, I was upon seeing Koshen there.

"Indeed, I did Kovak. What it is that requires my presence this early?" I asked as Koshen looked on with a dubious look on his face.

"There is talk the humans are planning to attack us. When? We do not know. However, their reason for this is there has been an increase in the number of human killings in the past six months. Upon hearing the news, Tazar and I decided to see for ourselves if there were any truth to what the humans were saying. Tell him what we found," he said to Tazar.

"The bite marks and treatment of the bodies were more than similar to ours; they were ours; which means there are some amongst us who refuse to follow the rules of the coven."

"This is serious. Our battles with humans have lessened since our plans were put into effect several years ago. This will surely set us back and put us in an uncomfortable position," I stated.

"Agreed, and I need you to put a small group together and find out who the culprits are. I want you in charge. Is that clear?" Kovak said to me.

"Yes."

"They will regret the day they disobeyed my words. Koshen will go along with you as well." He showed no emotion as Kovak continued. "Even those in the group should not be exempt from scrutiny."

"I will make sure of that," I assured him.

After everyone had left the room, I told Kovak of my suspicion the previous night. And despite telling him that I encountered a wild animal, I could tell from his demeanor that he was extremely concerned.

"I think you should be more watchful and if you notice anything unusual, please notify me."

"I will."

Later that evening, I confided in Benjamin and updated him on the adversities that we faced. He mentioned that he had also heard several disturbing sounds from his bedroom.

"What did it sound like?" I asked him.

"It sounded like a young girl and at other times it sounded like someone feasting on a meal. I have heard it the past few nights."

"The feasting I heard, and I ventured outside on a few occasions, but I didn't see anything unusual, so I left it alone. But now that you have mentioned it, I'll be ready the next time."

"Same here, I'll be on the lookout."

"Good, keep me informed. Have you heard anyone talking about humans getting killed?"

"No, but if I do, I'll let you know."

"I want you to be my other set of eyes and ears. This could lead to disaster if it continues."

"I know. I need to ask you this though."

"Go on."

"I never knew you were this bright. When did you get so bright? You the first . . . no, no, I wasn't gonna say that," he said almost apologetically, hoping I wouldn't take it personal. I told him, he had nothing to worry about. "I just wanted to let you know that I'm on your side. And it's not because you're the first Negro I know that's smart."

Laughing, I said, "Why thank you, Benjamin, especially since you put it that way."

"I'm glad we are friends."

"I feel the same," I said, knowing that I had an ally that I could count on. "We'll meet up in the study later tonight."

"I'll be there."

***

I sighed inwardly as I made my way to Kovak's study, knowing that we were at a crossroad that could determine our fate. He had given me a personal key to come and go as I pleased. I was the only one given this special privilege. I immersed myself tremendously in my studies. It would have been unimaginable for me to have continued living as a human under the conditions that I did, without reading and continuing some form of studious intellectual work.

Now and then Kovak would stop in and greet me in one of the many languages. I obliged him by continuing the conversation, which pleased him a lot. A few hours later, I had concluded my studies and met with Ravina in her room. She wasn't aware of the recent killings and as I confided in her, I told her not to say a word. She promised that she wouldn't.

"Good. Have you noticed anything odd of late?"

"No, and what do you mean by odd?"

"Any strange noise, any strangers, or suspicious behavior from the others?"

"No, I haven't. But if I do see or hear anything suspicious, I'll let you know."

"Good. Do you recall the night at the ball?"

"Go on."

"Well, after my encounter with Koshen, he whispered something in your sister's ear and then left the room."

"Oh? And what was her reaction, if any?"

"Honestly, there wasn't one."

"But it's bothering you?"

"Yes, so many things are happening right now. And I'm a firm believer that what you don't know, can and will hurt you if you sit back and do nothing."

"I understand. I'll see if I can get her to tell me what he said. Would that help?"

"Of course, it would."

"Come, let's go to the study. Are you going to play the piano tonight?"

"Not tonight, my dear. Benjamin and I have some things to take care of."

"You do know that I love how you play, right? So, tell me, what am I going to do if you decide not to?" she asked, smiling.

"It won't work. But I'll say this much, do what you have always done," I teased her.

"That's not fair," she said pouting. I held her hand as we walked to the study.

That's odd, I said to myself, entering the study. Benjamin never showed. Koshen greeted me as if the encounters we had, had never occurred. Savina did likewise. I kept my eyes on them the whole time. Nothing unusual happened. We had a wonderful time and like I promised Ravina, I did not play the piano.

EPISODE
10

As I lay in bed that night, the sudden rustle of leaves and cracking of sticks aroused me. I sprang into action and was quickly in the woods.

"Who goes there?" a voice said.

I turned around and it was Benjamin. "It's me, and what are you doing out here?" I said to him.

"I was about to lay down when I heard a noise coming from the woods. And I came out to see what it was."

"I heard the same thing as well. It looks like we're the only ones who heard it."

"It looks like it."

"Oh, we were supposed to meet in the study. Weren't we?"

"I know. But I followed Isabel into town, and we didn't get back until it was midnight."

I laughed. "Midnight? We are the undead. Midnight is when we actually should be on the prowl."

"But weren't you the one who said that we are a different breed?" he laughed.

"You are right. But Kovak doesn't allow anyone to be outside that time of the night, unless we are taking care of business, especially with the killings of the humans."

"Isabel said he gave her permission and she wanted company, so I went along."

"I understand. Let's go inside."

Benjamin's behavior at times was troubling and unexplained. Yet it wasn't as overbearing as Koshen's. I had always expected the best in him, despite his immaturity at times, as opposed to the worst of Koshen. The hair on my head would stand on its own at times when I encountered him.

My conversations with Benjamin were always straightforward and I would question him on how he felt about certain members of the coven and would he defend his kind at all costs. To which he would reply without hesitation that he would rather die a vampire's death, defending our kind. I had anticipated him sharing some mysterious, dark, and disturbing secrets with me, only because Isabel had replaced Savina as Kovak's lover.

Yet, that was never the case, because there was nothing to be told that would have slandered or vilified my maker. As one of the high-ranking undead and having to answer to Kovak, a position which I assumed with pride and respect, it was my responsibility and duty to prevent the groundwork of our ancestors, our Council, our coven, and the Argi from annihilation from enemies within and outside our coven.

Although Kovak was passionately in love with Isabel, I doubted if he was pleased upon her return that night, knowing how observant and unnerved the humans had become. Benjamin never told me the reason for her going into town. Nonetheless, I promised myself that whatever concerns I had about Isabel; I would bring them to Kovak's attention when the time was right.

With such a large number of vampires in our coven, the likelihood of dissent was possible. Whenever there's a considerable number of members in any organization there are some who will not always agree with the leadership. Aware of this, Kovak dealt harshly with those who would question his, the Council, and especially the Argi's authority.

Those lucky enough to stay alive after crossing Kovak welcomed the idea of banishment from the coven, instead of entering their eternal paradise. Betraying one's coven was the worst kind of treachery any vampire would want to be known for. Along with Benjamin and Koshen, I saw to it that those who put up any form of resistance were brought before the Argi. At least that was something the three of us had in common.

***

A few months had passed, and except for the nightly disturbances in the woods and solving who was behind the killings of the humans, it was clear to everyone that they were off-limits, unless we were provoked. Kovak was pleased otherwise and hinted that even the shrewd and cunning Trajar has been silent for some time and that might be a sign of good things to come.

"You think so?" I asked him one night as he hosted a small gathering for one of our allies, who had replaced his father as leader of their coven.

"Ah, at times I do my son. Yet I am aware of his treachery. But it's been a while since we last heard anything."

"I understand, but let's not lose sight of the fact that you and Tazar know him better than anyone else. Therefore, I beg to differ with your earlier statement."

Laughing, he said, "My son, you know me well. At times I want to believe that we can live peacefully. But you are right. I do know him best." He continued laughing as we toasted the young man.

As faith would have it, the peace that Kovak and the others yearned for was quickly thwarted, when the young, but beautiful Tana and Kovak's assistant was viciously attacked and killed by several of Trajar's fighters. She was accompanied by Koshen's two male friends, and their account of what happened left a lot of unanswered questions.

Ironically enough, they made it back to the coven with only a few scratches. Kovak was furious as they explained themselves. He and a group of us went to the location where she was attacked.

Kovak let out a loud emotional hiss before saying, "Look at what they did to her!!!" He flew in a rage and pinned the two against a tree. He was about to rip their heads from their bodies, but Koshen pleaded with him to spare them. It was only when Tazar approached and whispered in his ear, did he release them. Trajar and his fighters had ripped her skin and her head from her body. It was a gruesome sight. A wave of emotions hit me as I wondered how she must have felt. I stared at the two, ready to attack. Useless, they are not worthy to be vampires or of this coven, I said to myself.

"We are sorry," both stammered.

"Why didn't you remain and fight alongside her?" Kovak snarled.

"We did. We fought, but they outnumbered us," the taller of the two vampires said.

"We did Kovak, but when Trajar appeared she went after him and for a moment we couldn't see her," the other vampire said.

"Gather her up," he commanded them. "We are not leaving her here."

The mood was still somber days later. It seemed as if things were spiraling out of control. It was a daunting task for some members to digest, knowing that it could have been any one of them. The thought of a brother or sister leaving you behind in a life-and-death battle was difficult to handle.

Kovak was still grieving but was able to prepare and discuss our plan of attack and when we would do so. He had the full support of the Council and the Argi.

***

I was unsettled that night as I lay in bed. I decided to take a walk, and as I made my way through the garden, I heard a rustle. I stood in the dark ready to pounce upon whatever or whoever it was when my smell quickly alerted me to someone from our coven. I stood my ground knowing that if I ventured too far, whoever it is might pick up my scent and flee. I couldn't believe what I was seeing. It was a young girl. She was at least fifteen or sixteen years old. Benjamin was right about hearing the voice of a girl; and why didn't I pick up her scent? I asked myself. The scent was still strong, but it wasn't of the young girl.

She was feasting on the blood of some wild animal. Oblivious to my presence. The smell of my coven filled my nostril once again and to my amazement, Isabel and Savina appeared. My anticipation was heightened as I wondered if they were going to attack the girl. I wanted to question her. So, I waited. I was ready to intervene as they looked around aware that someone from the coven was nearby.

"Come here, Nalia," I heard Savina say in a whisper. They knew her. How could this be? I asked myself.

"But I'm still hungry," the girl replied.

"I have enough here for you, come," Isabel added, urging her on. Isabel and Savina? How could this be? I thought.

She released the carcass of the animal and Isabel handed her a small pouch filled with blood. She put it in her mouth and quickly gulped it down. She reached for the pouch that Savina held and did the same. I was at a loss for words. I couldn't fathom why I couldn't pick up on her scent. It was obvious she wasn't from our ally's coven. It was a mystery, as I watched them. They walked to the other side of the garden. I heard the dragging of feet and other movements; the scent of our coven traveled through my thoughts once again. It was Benjamin.

"What are you doing out here?" I said.

"I heard noises and I came to see what it was."

"I just got here myself. Did you see anything?"

I wasn't going to share what I saw with him at least not at that moment. Secondly, the women's scent no longer lingered and this troubled me. I had no idea where they went. I thought about reaching out to them, but I feared they would figure out that it was me in the garden. But they had to know that someone saw or at least heard them. I said to myself. How could they not have picked up my scent, or they just didn't care?

"No, but I picked up our coven smell as soon as I entered the garden. I figured it was you. Did you see anything?"

I laughed softly and said, "I guess we are the only ones trying to figure this thing out, huh? I didn't see a thing either."

"It's strange, Salas, some nights you hear it and at other times you don't. I don't like it."

"I feel the same way. But tonight, it was in the garden. Normally, it would come from the woods."

"I know. I looked in the woods a few nights ago and saw the dead bodies of several animals. What kind of animal does that?"

I smiled to myself upon hearing him say that. It was obvious that he hadn't looked at us, the undead in the same light. But aren't we the same as the four-legged animals that he thinks sucked the blood from those carcasses and left them there? Should he be surprised when he finds out that it was done by one of the undead, although not from our coven?

EPISODE
11

I was more than eager to sit down and talk to Kovak. And after being summoned to his library, I was readily prepared for him to shed some light on whatever it was that he wanted to talk about. I had a few questions of my own. What's more, I decided that I wasn't going to say a word about the occurrences that took place in the garden at least not at that moment. I was willing to wait and see whether Isabel and Savina would mention it. We greeted each other and after discussing the day's events and other important issues, I wanted to know how close he and Tana were. So, I decided to take the initiative.

"I know this isn't any of my business, but you knew that Tana and I were good friends and . . ." He stopped me in mid-sentence.

"She was my niece. It was a cruel fate how she became a vampire. Her parents were murdered by a band of thieves, who saw them as rich aristocrats. I was already one of the undead, and it was only because I would stand in the distance and wish I were still human that brought me there that fateful night. I watch my brother's family earlier that night, but my thirst was overwhelming me, and I decided to feed myself. Something stirred deep within me as I headed back to my coven. In those days, humans had a passion to destroy us even more so than they do today. We traveled as a group and my coven was against me traveling alone.

No sooner than I return to my brother's home, the fresh smell of blood greeted me. There wasn't any scent of another vampire, and as I entered, my brother and his wife lay dead. Their two sons had also met the same fate. They were savagely butchered. Seeing this pained me. It was as if I had become something else.

I noticed Tana sitting on the floor, wide-eyed and staring at me. She had never seen me before. I didn't know what to do. I couldn't take her with me to the coven. They would have devoured her. I couldn't allow her to become an orphan either. So, I made the cruel decision to make her one of the undead." I sat there enthralled by what he told me. Even as he spoke, you could see the pain in his steel-hardened black eyes. "She meant everything to me. I promised her that I would never leave her side and that she would be with me forever. I failed her."

"It wasn't your fault. It was out of your control."

"My son, what do I do now?"

"You live. You continue."

"Ah, isn't it ironic that you would be telling this old vampire to live and continue? But you're right. We have to continue the work of our makers and see to it that our coven remains strong."

"Indeed, Kovak." At the end of our conversation, I walked to the study. I quickly picked up from where I had left off and delved into my studies as a man possessed.

***

I later met up with Ravina. I was hoping that she might have heard something concerning the young girl. It seemed she was clueless, and it reassured me that Savina hadn't said a word. I asked her if she knew that Tana was Kovak's niece. And she said, yes.

"It took me all these years to find out they were related," I said.

"Kovak rarely talks about his family. In all the years that Savina and I have been around him, I doubt if he ever mentioned them more than once."

"Hmm, he's very secretive, huh?"

"I wouldn't say that."

"No? Then what would you say?"

"I think if you were to ask him about certain things, he would give you an answer."

"I'll remember that."

"At times, he can be bossy. Don't you think so?"

"Not at all! I would say demanding, but certainly not bossy. His leadership skills are unparalleled, and you have to be demanding at times to get things done."

"He sure was bossy at the outset. He has calmed down over the years. He's more melancholy in his old age," she said, laughing.

"You believe what you're saying?"

"Yes, I do."

"I guess I came at the right time then, huh?" I remarked.

"You sure did."

She held me close and kissed me, ignoring the fact that although we were in the library, we could be seen by the others, who giggled and snickered as they passed by. I was shy and would rather do things in private than out in the open. She would remind me that she would continue to work on my shyness. I laughed at her suggestions.

"Still haven't heard anything from your sister?"

"No, I haven't."

"Did you ask?"

"Yes, but she said she couldn't recall."

I wonder why I said to myself.

"Don't worry about it. If she recalls and tells you, I would like to know."

"Sure."

I kissed her and said goodnight. As I made my way through the huge hallways, I bumped into Kovak and Tazar.

"Ah, there my son, you look a bit tired. Not getting enough sleep?" Kovak said as both men laughed. I couldn't help myself but join them. "I thought we weren't supposed to get tired. Right, Tazar? I can't put my finger on it, but I think I know why." They both looked at each other with a slight smile.

"It could be that I'm getting old like you two."

"Old?" Tazar said aloud. "I guess you must be referring to Kovak."

"Speak for yourself," Kovak shot back as we continued laughing. He then added, "The humans have started complaining once again. Did you find out anything since the last time we spoke?"

"Not much, but Benjamin has been looking into some things for me."

"Wonderful! Well, Tazar and I shall be on our way."

Both men had a sense of humor which was refreshing given all they had been through. Their friendship seemed genuine, and they were constantly together, rarely did you see one without the other.

***

It was early in the morning, and I was sitting in the living quarters drinking a glass of the finest human blood; when Savina came and sat down next to me. I was quite surprised. She had a smile on her face and for what it was worth; the air around her gave off a breath of fresh air.

"How are you?"

"I'm fine and you?"

"Wonderful!" I felt some apprehension as she began talking. "I heard you have been looking into the killings of the humans. How are things going? What has your investigation proved or gotten you so far?"

Smiling, I said, "It's really difficult to say right now."

"And why is that?"

"Mostly everyone is being uncooperative."

"Is that so?"

"Indeed."

"Perhaps, you'll get some cooperation shortly."

"From you? I look forward to it."

Laughing, she said, "Possibly, you never know."

"I hope so."

"Oh, how are things coming along with you and Ravina?"

"Wonderful."

"Fantastic," she said, before hurrying off and saying something about meeting up with Kovak. No sooner than I had done talking to Savina, a cautious-looking Benjamin approached me.

"We need to talk," he said.

"About?"

"A lot, but not here!"

I was walking to one of the rooms, but he kept insisting that there was something that he had to show me. Benjamin and I lifted in the frigid winter air, which we were immune to. There was ice all over the landscape and the frostiness and the biting wind made the few humans that we saw along the way, cringe under the coldness. We maneuvered our way through the skies as we avoided the prying eyes of the humans.

"Did you hear the commotion last night?" Benjamin asked.

"No, I did not. Why? What happened?"

"Veech and Zan are no longer amongst us."

"What do you mean?" The two were the ones who left a helpless Tana alone with the murdering Trajar and his coven.

"I was restless and decided to do some reading."

"Reading? You?"

"If you must know our library on the farmhouse back when I was a human held a lot of books. And I read a lot."

KARL ANTHONY

Chuckling, as I watched the ground below us, I said, "I believe you."

"Seem you don't, ask my sister."

"I will," I added just so he would continue.

"As I was reading, I heard a thumping noise. I got up and began following the sound. But the closer I would get; the sound would move ahead of me. I followed it to a part of the mansion I had never been to before. It was sealed off and I could hear the muffled sound of someone pleading."

"Hmm."

"I tried listening, but I couldn't get through. The hissing sounds were drowning out the muffled sound and I had a tough time hearing."

"You must show me this part of the mansion that you speak of," I said, as we descended to the ground gracefully.

"Then it got quiet, and I heard the slamming of a door. I knew whoever it was had taken off. I still couldn't make out who it was or what it was until I decided to look for myself, and this is what I found." He took me to an isolated area that humans could never gain access to; you had to be one of the undead.

The bodies were headless, mutilated, and burnt. I was beyond disbelief. I couldn't find the right words, to sum up how I felt. According to Benjamin, they were destroyed at the mansion and their burnt remains were dumped at the very spot. It had to be the work of Kovak and Tazar. No one else would be brave enough to do such things. But how would I approach Kovak about this or should I just leave it alone? I thought.

"I don't know what to say."

"Aren't you going to find out who did it? We need to know. It could happen to any of us. This isn't how it's supposed to be, is it, Salas?"

"No, you're right; it's not supposed to be this way. Come, let us go."

Once again, I found myself in an unusual position. Kovak would expect me to bring this to his attention, especially if it ends up hurting our coven. He would certainly look at me in a different light if I didn't say anything and things turn out differently, and this was something that I wasn't willing to risk. Benjamin and I arrived just in time to greet Kovak and the others. They were in the guest room. Kovak was sitting at the piano as I approached.

"You look troubled, come," he said. I whispered in his ear that we needed to talk. "As soon as I'm done with this selection, I have never heard you play this before."

"I promise you; I will play it tomorrow."

Minutes later, Kovak and I were in his private library.

"What is so important that you dragged me away from my music?"

"It's Veech and Zan; they are no longer amongst us."

"What? What are you talking about? Who told you this?"

"No one told me. I saw their burnt remains with my own eyes."

"Where is it? Come, show me." I took him to where the ashy remains were. "Was it Benjamin who told you of this?" I stuttered. "So how did you know where the remains were? What did you hear or see?"

"I cannot lie to you. It was him."

"What did he see or hear?"

"He didn't see anything. He said he heard strange sounds, but they were muffled. And he couldn't get a breakthrough."

"I see. So, he brought it to your attention. Why didn't you inform me immediately?"

"I would have, but he didn't come outright and tell me. He said he wanted to show me something and I followed."

"Say no more my son, I understand. Gather the others and meet me in the main room."

He abruptly left the library. If Kovak was the one to have done this, he certainly didn't act like it. I told Benjamin what transpired and as I expected, he was beside himself as he wondered if Kovak would punish him. I assured him that I didn't get that from our conversation. I told him that he was visibly upset, to which Benjamin let out a loud worried sigh.

"Come, let's go and tidy ourselves. We are expected in the main room along with the others."

EPISODE

12

"What is going on? What is happening?" several members of the rank and file asked.

"I don't know," I replied.

"What is it that you have stirred up now?" Koshen said, without looking at me.

"Something I should have done a long time ago," I said, snatching him by the neck.

"No," a voice yelled out, as Tazar in a flash pulled my hand from his throat.

"I guess somebody woke up on the wrong side this morning, huh?" Koshen said nonchalantly, heaving his shoulder up and down as if he was trying to show me up.

KARL ANTHONY

Without warning, Kovak's eloquent and cadence voice took center stage.

"As some of you may know, there was a situation that took place last night. For those of you who weren't briefed, you will be in a few minutes."

It was a moderate number of members inside the room. Some of the faces were familiar to me. They were mostly members of the Council and the Argi. I could feel their eyes penetrating my every move as they glanced at me. The room was calm as they listened to Kovak.

"It was brought to my attention not too long ago that Veech and Zan are no longer with us." Koshen immediately turned and stared in my direction. "It seems there were some unauthorized activities that took place last night. No one is going to use the death of Tana, as a means by which to earn my respect by savagely murdering those two. If anyone was supposed to take those measures, it should have been me. Let me make this clear, something went wrong. I don't know who committed this depraved act, but whoever it was or were; they were quite familiar with our mansion and were in an off-limits area. Mark my words; the culprit will not go unpunished. We will find out who you are, and you will be dealt with accordingly," he finished up.

"Why do I feel like you had something to do with it, huh?" Koshen said to me, before walking out of the main room.

Overhearing what he said, Tazar responded, "Pay him no mind, he's just upset because they were close."

"I know."

"Excuse me, Salas!"

74

"Sure," I said, as Tazar made his way over to the table. There Kovak was having a conversation with members of the Argi. As I stood to the side, Ravina approached me. She had a concerned look on her face as I began telling her what happened.

"This is frightening and unacceptable. Someone here is responsible, and we need to find out who it is," she said with a displeased look on her face.

"I'm in total agreement with you. Kovak appears to be stunned that Tana was taken from him and maybe, perhaps, I don't know . . ."

She immediately cut me off, and said, "Assumptions are for idiots, are you one?"

"No," I responded in a defensive tone. I was startled. "I was only trying to make a point."

"You are talking about our leader, our maker. You should be glad that you are sharing these things with me and not someone else. They would have told him by now."

"Perhaps, you are right."

"It's not perhaps, my love, I am right. You could be banished or destroyed for making such a claim. I have been with him a long time and despite his ways at times, I will stake my life on it that he wasn't the one."

"Hmm, then there is no need for me to say any more about this. Come, let's go to town, I need to clear my thoughts."

***

KARL ANTHONY

What Ravina said made lots of sense and the more I thought about it, I was glad I never mentioned it to anyone else. I intended to only take into consideration the events leading up to their death. Was I suggesting that Kovak did it? No. I knew he was a man of high standards and integrity, but at what price did he lead his coven? And had I admired him to such an extent that my loyalty towards him overshadowed everything else, that I would foolishly follow his commands blindly? I hesitated to think of all those things as Ravina and I blended in nicely with the humans as we walked the streets of Leicester.

Moments later, our pleasant walk was interrupted by the scent of some unknown coven. It was powerful and overbearing, which indicated to us that there were at least five or six strangers, and the one giving off the strongest scent was the leader. To our dismay, the streets were filled with people shopping and chatting, and without the slightest clue of the danger that lurked.

"They had to have picked up our scent as well," Ravina said as we kept our eyes on the crowd.

"I'm quite sure they did. I wonder who it is, and why would they show up here, if not to feed on the humans?"

I was awaiting Ravina's response when she suddenly released my hand and inched closer to the curb as a horse and wagon slowly made their way down the street towards us.

"It's getting stronger," she said.

"It is. I can taste it. How much money do you have with you?"

"Money? Why?"

"Do you?"

"Yes."

"Give it to me. You see that costume store across the street?"

"Yes."

"I'm going to get us some costumes, masks, whatever."

"What for?"

"We live here. We can't afford to challenge whoever it is and stay in Leicester. The humans will know it's us, and let's not forget the sun is still out."

"Hurry then, Salas, I will keep an eye on them."

I couldn't move at my normal pace. I had to be mindful of that as I strolled across the street like a normal human and entered the store. The stranger's scent was now much stronger and as the kind gentleman inside the store looked at me with wary eyes, I immediately pretended as if I was back at the Big House. I told him my master had sent me. He handed me the costumes and masks. I paid him and cautiously crossed the street and approached Ravina, who was ready for battle. The humans had no inkling of what was about to transpire.

"Come, put it on here," I said, pulling her off to the side.

With our faces now covered and dressed in the costumes, we had to act fast. We swooped down on the horse and wagon at blinding speed. The driver immediately attacked us as the others revealed themselves. We had to get them away from humans.

Ravina and I took to the skies with them in pursuit. The humans were clueless as they looked around. The only indication of something strange taking place was the horse and wagon veering out of control without a driver.

KARL ANTHONY

"I'll take them to where Veech and Zan were destroyed. Follow me." Ravina was powerful and at times flew ahead of me. "Here, over there."

The hissing was loud enough to drive any human crazy as we prepared for battle. Ravina then said, "It's six of them and two of us, I can tell that only the leader is old. The others are young."

"Yes, I sensed that also," I said in return as they swooped down on us.

I viciously attacked the leader and the two males he was with. Ravina attacked the three females. It was a fierce battle as we fought for our lives. I ripped apart the first young vampire, bending and breaking his body over several three branches. Ravina called out to me, and as I looked over at her, she was pinned to the ground, and they were about to rip her apart. I swooped down on them with the two males in pursuit, when without warning; Koshen appeared out of nowhere and ripped apart the necks of two of the females.

I was thankful that he showed up. Ravina then tore apart the lone female as she shrieked from her limbs being shredded to pieces. The three of us then attacked the others. We immediately destroyed the other male and captured the leader. He pleaded with us to destroy him, but we would have none of it. We needed to know why he was in Leicester, and as we made our way back to the coven with our prisoner; Koshen and I didn't say a word.

I could hear the hissing of our coven members reverberating around us as the mansion came into view. My companions were able to smell the stench of our prisoner as we got closer. Since I became one of the undead, the town of Leicester had been a haven for our kind. Thus, the intense stench of the unknown brought Kovak and the others to the terraces and the courtyard. Everyone stood still as Kovak approached with a somber, yet stern look on his face.

"Who is this?" he asked me.

"He and his kind were in a fierce battle with Salas and Ravina when I showed up and rescued them," Koshen interject, before I or Ravina could respond.

"Is that so, Salas?"

"Don't believe a word of what he said," Ravina answered. She and I told Kovak what had transpired, and as he listened, Koshen was about to interrupt our conversation when in the blink of an eye, a visibly upset Tazar snatched him by the throat and told him to remain quiet.

"Bring the prisoner in," Kovak said. He turned and signaled to Tazar, who told the others to carry on as they were before. With the Argi accompanying us, we entered an area that was unfamiliar to me. As I walked on with the others, I thought, could this be the place that Benjamin told me about?

We walked down a dimly lit corridor and entered a huge area where a huge steel door was opened by several of our most dedicated kind. I too was taken aback by their appearances. I rarely saw them with the others. As I looked on, I was more than convinced that this was the place where Veech and Zan were first taken and destroyed.

Our prisoner was hissing loudly, and his piercing eyes were filled with hate. He stared at Kovak and Tazar before turning his gaze towards me, Ravina and Koshen. He slowly lifted his head and began talking. I quickly recognized that he was talking in Anatolian. Kovak and Tazar stared at each other before signaling for the guards to chain him. The

Argi was deeply interested to hear what he had to say as well. Ravina and Koshen along with the guards were the only ones unaware of what was being said.

"This is how I finally get to meet Kovak and Tazar, the two most despised vampire killers," he snarled.

"Who are you and what is your name?" Kovak asked him.

"I'm called, Adan."

"Where did you learn to speak this tongue and who taught you it?"

"Wouldn't you like to know?" he scoffed.

Reaching for his sword which he always kept on his side, Kovak meticulously began slicing his body as sulfuric ash emerged from the open wounds. It was the sword he has fought with since he became one of the undead. The pain was overwhelming our prisoner and as he screamed out in anguish, Kovak let out a pleasing laugh.

"Are you ready to answer the question now?"

"It was Trajar. Please! Please!"

"Where is he?"

"He has left these lands and has returned to the Old World."

"When shall he return?"

"He never said. Destroy me now!" he pleaded.

"How dare you come here and attack humans. Was it your assignment to turn them against us? Isn't that why you were ordered here?" Tazar demanded. I had never seen Tazar behave in this manner before.

"We didn't come to attack the humans. We came for the girl."

"What girl?" Kovak asked with raised eyebrows.

"Her, the one we attacked," he said, pointing at Ravina. She gasped as she wondered why Trajar would come after her.

"We are going to destroy you and your coven one by one. Trajar will get her eventually. She's . . ."

He couldn't complete his sentence as Kovak threw his sword at his neck slicing it from the rest of his body. The Argi smiled and so did Kovak, Tazar, and Koshen. I managed to display a half-smile not because he was killed. I was curious to hear what else he had to say.

EPISODE
13

"How dare you to lie to Kovak about what happened?" Ravina snapped at Koshen.

"It was the truth."

"The truth? You stood there and lied. Fortunately, neither Kovak nor Tazar believed you. It is beyond me as to why you would carry on this way."

He was about to respond when Ravina let out a low hiss, revealing her fangs. I had never seen her behave in this manner towards him. She was angry.

"I saved your life, didn't I? If I weren't there you wouldn't be here disrespecting me."

"You did nothing of the sort. I was doing fine."

"Surely, you were. Our relationship means a lot to me, and I couldn't allow it to happen."

"There is nothing between you and me, whatever we had before Salas's, is over."

"How could you choose him over me? He's new to our coven, can't you see that? Did you tell him? Did you?"

"You know nothing. My heart is with Salas, and we are happy. There's nothing to tell."

"You will not do this to me. You will not humiliate me in front of everyone."

"Everyone? It is only you and I talking."

Unsuspectingly, I stood off to the side watching and listening. I was by no means being ungrateful, quite the contrary, because he did save her from significant injury or death. However, his lying to Kovak is what bothered me.

In the same breath, I wanted to know what he was doing when the bodies of Veech and Zan were dumped. Wanting an answer, I exposed myself and pretended as if I had just stumbled upon them.

Before I could say a word, Koshen smiled and said, "She is yours, congratulation. She has made it known to me that you are the one she's chosen for all eternity. You have won," he finished up as Ravina looked on.

Unfazed by his words, I did however acknowledge him and then pursued to ask him what he was doing at the site to which he answered, "They were my friends, and I loved them as much as they loved me. I had to see where their remains were dumped. I saw them the night before and we laughed and talked about our early days as naive young men, who drove everyone insane. That's the reason why I was there, to say goodbye to my friend, Salas. Have you ever lost anyone close to you? Oh, never mind, yes you did, your beloved, Evelyn," he finished up, before walking away.

I stood there speechless as he disappeared from my sight. I was puzzled by what it was that Ravina hadn't shared with me. Still, I was confident that she would. His mention of Evelyn surprised me, and although it was mute as far as I was concerned, it was hurtful and done deliberately and directed at Ravina more so than at me.

"The nerve of him, I can't stand him," Ravina said with disdain.

"I must say, it was a nice try on his part, but leave it alone."

"I will, but only because of you."

"Wonderful, I appreciate it. Still, haven't heard from your sister?"

"No, I haven't. But I must say, she's been acting strange of late."

"Oh, she is, huh?"

"Yes, and Benjamin has been snooping around a lot lately." Ravina had no idea that he was doing so on my behalf, and I was optimistic upon hearing this. It proved that he was doing exactly as I asked of him.

"Hmm, I see. I wouldn't pay too much attention to Benjamin. He's just the inquisitive type, that's all."

Laughing, she said, "He does act like it."

"Come," I said to her as we made our way to her chamber. The day had been long and incredibly eventful and what started as a pleasant day for me and Ravina ended with more drama than either of us could have ever anticipated.

***

I was up and about early the following morning, and as I stared at Ravina as she brushed her hair, I was taken by how beautiful she was. I was mesmerized by her beauty. She was simply irresistible, and I couldn't help myself. I approached her from behind and held her around the waist. I was quite confident about her one day becoming my wife. I dismissed Koshen and everything that he represented because he wasn't an honest suitor, hence the reason for Ravina's decision to no longer be with him.

As lovers, our lives were linked through our genuine love for each other and to share and live it freely. It was a love that was neither insincere nor superficial. Ravina turned and smiled at me. Our eyes were filled with passion and as they lit up, I felt that urge, that rush, once again. It was a wonderful and touching moment as she reached for my face and slowly ran her fingers over it.

I could no longer control how I felt. And as I stared into her beautiful eyes, I slowly lowered my head and kissed her soft lips. She reciprocated and as our tongues explored each other's mouth, I pulled her closer as her stiff young breast rubbed against my chest, buckling my already weaken knees. Our kiss deepened, and as I lifted her and moved her dress to the side, and entered her. Our mouths opened, exposing our fangs as we grazed them against our flesh. I ran my hands through her hair as she held me around the neck and rode me into eternal bliss, hissing, and licking each other's faces.

"That was unbelievable, Salas!"

"Hmm, you were unbelievable yourself."

"You do it to me every time. No one has ever made me feel this way. You were great."

"You said no one? Does that mean . . ."

Cutting me off, she smiled shyly, "Yes, better than he ever was."

"It's the things you do to me."

"What have I done?" she giggled.

"Never mind!"

"No, no, continue! I want to hear."

"Your movements and the things you do are what drive me to that point." I laughed aloud. She couldn't help herself as she began laughing as well. Our laughter was suddenly interrupted by a knock on the door.

"Who is it?" she asked.

"It's me, Savina."

"Just a minute," she said, fixing her dress and hair.

"Oh, hello, Salas," Savina said, upon entering the room.

"Hi!" I replied.

"I'm so sorry for barging in on you and Ravina without warning. I'll return another time."

"No, it's fine. I was leaving anyway."

"You are?" Ravina asked.

"Yes, my dear. I'll return later." I left the sisters alone, knowing that I wouldn't let the day end without bringing up the incident in the garden with Savina.

***

After leaving Ravina's side, I continued my studies and ventured into town with Benjamin, who insisted that I go with him. On the way, we talked about the incident with Trajar's lackeys and how Koshen had done so much damage to his reputation than he could have ever imagined. The conversation soon changed to Benjamin's reasons for wanting me to accompany him into town.

"So why did you insist on me coming along?"

"I met this girl. She's really beautiful and I wanted you to meet her."

"Really?" I was puzzled as to why he would want to see someone else outside of our coven. Surely, there were some beautiful women within our coven. "It's obvious she's not one of ours. Is it fair to say so?"

"Yes," he said, sounding unsure.

"So which coven is she from? Hopefully, she isn't from one of our nemesis."

"No, no, she's not."

"So, go on."

"She's human," he answered, stroking his chin as he eagerly awaited my response.

"Human? What in the world were you thinking?"

"What do you mean?"

"Does she know who you are?"

"No, she doesn't."

"I don't know, Benjamin. I don't know. Are you two serious about each other, or is it one of those things?"

"I love her, Salas."

"This is a rather difficult one to assess. You're one of the undead. She will live and die as a human, then what?"

"I'm aware of this, and this is why I wanted your opinion."

KARL ANTHONY

"My opinion?"

"Yes."

"About?"

"What I should do."

"Meaning?"

"Should I tell her who I am, or should I take her with me forever?"

"This I will have to think about."

"I brought you along because I want you to meet her. I told her about you."

"You did, and what did you say exactly?" I asked, curiously.

"That you are my best friend and how great of a fella you are."

"Well, at least that's good to know. I'll meet her."

"Come then, she lives just beyond the haberdashery."

"Is she the reason why you accompanied your sister to town? And please do not lie. I know that you two have been coming into town quite frequently."

"Yes, you're correct, but it was Isabel who introduced me to her."

"Isabel was the one?"

"Yes."

"Does she know about Isabel?"

"No, she doesn't."

"Hmm, I see." We were a few feet from the house when a beautiful brunette walked out the front door. I understood why Benjamin was smitten.

"Madeline," Benjamin called. She turned and smiled at him, but her smile quickly faded when she noticed me standing there. "This is my friend, John, I was telling you about."

"How are you doing?" I said, extending my hand.

She immediately looked around making sure that no one was looking, before shaking my hand. It was a bit awkward, to say the least, but I understood.

"I'm doing fine," she quipped.

"Wonderful."

"Come in," she said to Benjamin ushering him inside.

Benjamin would have none of it. "John and I came together . . ."

Cutting him off, she warily looked around before ushering us both in.

"I meant you no disrespect," she said to me.

"I understand," I said to her reassuringly.

"Care for some beverage?" she asked.

Benjamin and I looked at each other and smiled, before telling her that we were fine. She never gave any indication as to whether she was offended by our refusal to drink. We spoke at length, and after an hour or so we headed home.

"So, what do you think?" Benjamin asked once we were back at the mansion.

"She's a nice girl. But I would always advise you to be cautious. You can never allow her or the other humans to know who you are, and this you must be mindful of at all times."

"You're right, and I will. I think she's captured my heart."

"It shows," I said. We laughed.

"I knew you would like her."

KARL ANTHONY

"Just be careful. On another note, Savina still hasn't mentioned a word about the incident in the garden. So, I have decided to bring it to her attention later today."

"Do you want me there?"

"Hmm, no, not at this moment, I'll let you know when."

"Not a problem. Well, I'll see you in the study in a few hours."

"I'll be there," I said, as I headed to my room. I had never brought it to Benjamin's attention that Isabel was with Savina in the garden that night, nor had I confronted Isabel about it. I would do so at the right time.

EPISODE
14

As darkness fell upon the town, I wasted no time in confronting Savina. I followed closely behind her as if minding my business, and as she departed Kovak's side and headed for the main guest room, I approached her.

"I knew you were following me, and for what may I ask?" she said, with a perturbed look on her face.

"I saw you and Isabel in the garden a while back and what I saw was rather interesting."

"What did you see, Salas?"

"I saw the girl, need I say more?"

Her eyes widened with concern as she pulled me to the side and said, "Come, we need to go elsewhere and talk." We made our way to the courtyard.

"Who is she? She's not of our coven and I couldn't detect her smell." I waited for an answer.

"Don't be alarmed because I didn't detect it either. I found her in the woods a few months ago. Where she's from? I don't know. The wind moves mysteriously and the undead follows the movement as they feed. She's no different."

"I understand. However, you never brought it to Kovak's attention, why?"

"Knowing Kovak, he might have destroyed her."

"How do you know such things?"

"Because I know him, he's done it before. Once you're not of our coven, he finds it difficult to keep you around. She's a child, Salas, a child."

"Where is she now?" She wouldn't say. "You have left me with no other choice other than to tell him. Where is she?" I demanded.

With a coy look on her face, she angrily replied, "She's here in my chambers."

I was stunned. "You have brought her into the coven without Kovak's permission? He knows?"

"Yes. He does. I told him that she doesn't remember a thing other than her name."

"But you just said he would have killed her, and now you're saying that you told him? What is it that I don't get?"

"What I meant to say is that it took me a while to convince him otherwise."

"Hmm! What is her name?"

I had already decided to sit down and talk with Kovak and the Argi about our new guest. I was baffled by the fact that neither he nor the Argi had mentioned anything about her.

"Her name is, Nalia."

"Hmm, but didn't it occur to you and Isabel that she and her kind might be the ones responsible for the killings of the humans?"

"Certainly, it did, but we were convinced that it wasn't her. If it was, where is her coven after all this time?"

"Who came upon her first, you or Isabel?"

"It was Isabel, and she told me about her."

"Isabel shared this information with you?"

"Yes, she did."

"The one who has stolen Kovak's heart, am I to believe this?"

"Stolen? She has not stolen his heart. I visit his chamber just as much as she does."

"And you're not a bit jealous?"

"No, Salas, I'm not."

"Why didn't you share it with your sister?"

"I didn't want to."

"Hmm, I see."

"And just so you know, Isabel and I talked about everything, and we are both comfortable with our situation."

"I wonder why, Savina?"

"It is obvious that you're looking for far more than what I can provide, therefore, I'll excuse myself."

I watched her as she made her way back inside the mansion. I was perplexed by the things she had said. I was trying to make sense of it all. She and Isabel's new-found friendship, I found strange. I was quite apprehensive and uneasy about, Nalia.

I entered the mansion and as I walked the halls, I headed for Kovak's study. I knew he would be up, and I was right. As I entered the study, there, he was with Isabel. He invited me to sit along with them. But I declined the offer and walked to the sitting area and sat with the others. I would wait until dawn to sit down with him. There were a few things on my mind that needed to be addressed. Who was Nalia and what if any situation would arise, how would we respond, in secrecy? I tried to remain positive.

***

I barely slept that night, and as dawn approached, I made my way to Kovak's section of the mansion. He was up early and as he greeted me, Isabel, aware of my presence, said hello, before leaving.

"I know what it is that has sparked your interest my dear, Salas. Is it not the young girl, Nalia?"

"Indeed. Aren't you a bit troubled by her mere presence and the way Isabel and Savina met her?"

"Certainly, I am. Her scent is not of our enemies that I can assure you."

"She does have a scent?"

"Yes, she does. Why do you ask such a question?"

"I came upon her, Savina and Isabel late one night and there wasn't a scent to her at all."

"I see. Nonetheless, if there wasn't a scent, I would not have allowed her to stay amongst us. But are you sure about that night?"

"Yes, I'm quite sure. There wasn't a scent to her. I'm puzzled by her appearance at this time, given the fact that we still haven't found out who is responsible for the death of the humans. It's also troubling that Savina told me that she was feeding on wild animals in the woods."

"What? Neither Savina nor Isabel had brought this to my attention," he said, his voice rising from his usually calm self. He let out a hiss and immediately, Isabel and Savina were in our presence. "What is this that Salas has informed me about Nalia feeding on wild animals in the woods?"

They were stunned, not because of the question itself, but the way he asked it. Their faces displayed fear and submissiveness as Savina responded, "Forgive me for not telling you of this. Salas is correct. We did find her out in the woods feeding on wild animals. It's my fault for not being more informative about what we saw."

"And you, my love?" he stared at Isabel with those cold dark eyes of his, as Savina looked on with an unpleasant look on her face.

"I thought it was brought to your attention . . ."

Cutting her off, he said, "You must be careful my love, and you Savina, this is not like you at all. I expected more from you and in the future, you both will do so. Is that clear?"

"Yes," they said in unison.

"Now, leave us! I think I should have another chat with our new guest, and I want you there, Salas."

"I'll be more than happy to be there. Are we going to talk to her now?"

"No, she is in our midst, so let's just keep our eyes on her. She is not strong enough to defend herself from any of us. If there's an ulterior motive for her being here, let's see how long before she reveals it, if there's one."

"Certainly!"

"Come, let's have a drink," he said, putting his arm around my shoulder.

EPISODE
15

I was pleased with Kovak's handling of the situation with Savina and Isabel. I was still disturbed by Benjamin's new human love interest. Yet Isabel's behavior and her frequent visit to town worried me, and I certainly didn't want Kovak to feel as if I was undermining and questioning his decisions. I hadn't brought it to his attention either. I felt I needed more time to at least investigate her reasons for going into town so often.

"Isabel," I called to her as she walked by my window one afternoon.

"Yes, Salas, how can I help you?"

"I need to ask you a question."

"Sure."

"You go to town quite a lot. I guess I must be missing all the fun, don't you think?"

Smiling, she replied, "Maybe you are. I would invite you, but you're quite busy and I wouldn't want to impose on your duties."

"Thank you for being so kind and considerate, but I will consider it." I wanted to ask her exactly what she did in town when she answered it for me.

"I'm friends with a few of the girls. Mostly everyone here is much older than me and I mean much older." She laughed. I couldn't agree more with her as I too began laughing.

"So, what do you and your friends do? I'm also assuming it was one of those friends that you introduce Benjamin to as well, is it?"

"We talk girl stuff," she said, giggling, "and admire the soldiers. Yes, I did introduce Madeline to my brother."

"You do know that you have to be very careful at all times, don't you?"

"Yes, I'm aware. I wouldn't do anything to jeopardize our coven and have the humans find us out; no, not ever."

"That is good. At the same time, I want you to be careful. Do you understand?"

"Yes, I understand." I ended the conversation. I was tempted to tell her not to say a word to Kovak. But I decided not to at the last minute.

***

The next day, I was summoned by Kovak and the Argi. There I met Nalia, only this time I immediately picked up her scent. She was a precocious girl and at times very playful. As I observed her, she seemed innocent as her large blue eyes seemed to paint a picturesque profile of my face.

"Hi, Nalia," I said.

"Hello, and how are you?"

"I'm fine."

"And your name?"

"I am, Salas."

"That is such a beautiful name."

"Thank you. Is there anything that you would like to share with me?"

"Yes."

"And what is that?" I asked as the others looked on curious as well.

"Thank you for having me," she giggled. We were all expecting to hear something else it seemed.

"Here," Kovak said, handing her a glass of the finest human blood. She put it to her head and gulped it down.

I spoke at length with her and at times she and I were left alone. I didn't suspect anything at all from our conversation. If anything, she reminded me of Isabel more than anything else, young and naive.

She later resumed playing with her playmates. We had a small number of young people amongst us that were turned by others of our covens who claimed they couldn't control their thirst. It was forbidden to turn children because they were defenseless against adult vampires who were much more powerful.

Kovak had made it known that young children were off-limits. He himself had turned a few young people when he first became one of the undead. You could hear the remorse in his voice whenever he talked about it. I think that played a role in the stance that he's now taken. Nevertheless, his orders were not overlooked or ignored. The fact is each situation differed one from the other and he understood.

"Listen," he said to me, "did you notice anything unusual about her scent?"

"No," I responded. "It hit me as soon as I entered the chamber."

"We will continue to play the waiting game. But eventually, I will have to decide as to whether she stays with us or not."

"What if we find out that she's an enemy of ours, what will become of her?"

Smiling, Kovak replied, "I will rip her apart limb by limb." I was taken aback not so much by him killing her, but by the tone of his voice and the way he gestured with his hands as he spoke.

"I see. I don't know what to say."

"My son, it shouldn't matter what your enemies look and sound like. Their sole purpose is to get in your midst and destroy you. I did it a few times as a young undead. You must always be prepared and ready. And when the time comes, you kill with a zeal that will send a message to your enemies." I listened to him intently. "Come along with me. I know you haven't found out as of this moment those responsible for the killings of the humans. I also know that Benjamin has been working alongside you. He wasn't just doing you a favor or helping you when he found time, right?"

"Did he tell you?"

He laughed. "No, my son, I am the immortal creature, Kovak. I know my coven. I am King of the Undead. Everything that I share with you, I do so because you are favored in my eyes. Do you understand?"

"Yes, I do."

"Carry on."

"I'm on a trail and hopefully it will lead me to those or the ones responsible for the killings, for which we are being blamed."

"Good. Now, there have been whispers of the humans preparing to fight amongst themselves once again."

"They are?"

"Yes, and I have spoken with the Council and the others, and I would like to know what you think. If the humans do indeed go to war, do you think we should help their cause by filling up our supplies while feeding on those on the battlefield?"

"That is brilliant," I smiled.

"So, you agree?"

"Yes, we should expand our supply at their expense. Surely, we aren't the ones pitting them against one another nor do we care what their quarrel is about, do we?"

Kovak laughed. "Come; let's have a drink, my son. We will drink to the humans and hope that they carry out their bitter quarrel and allow us to celebrate." I relished the moment, hoping we weren't under any false sense of security as we watched the humans escalate their war of words.

***

KARL ANTHONY

Kovak's words came to fruition as the humans had once again started another war. In 1861, the Civil War began with shots fired on Fort Sumter. The south became our feeding ground as we filled our supplies — taking them back to Massachusetts. We were pleased, as we fed on the supplies of blood. At times we were overwhelmed with the amount of food that was available to us. The humans were afraid and frightened once they realized that it wasn't just the soldiers on the battlefield that were dying. Those in the towns throughout Massachusetts were also dying at an alarming rate and they knew something or someone else was the cause.

My investigation into the killings of humans was no longer a priority at the initial outset of the war. Our focus was on the soldiers and the buildings and shacks where the bodies were kept. We filled our supplies and added several others to the mansion. Despite all this, the townspeople were still dying. Someone was still feasting on them despite the huge supplies and the soldiers that were available to us.

This drove the humans to attack us with a vengeance, unlike anything we had witnessed in some time. We fought, but they were relentless, and we lost several of our brothers and sisters. My suspicion was once again aroused as I began focusing on Nalia. Her behavior was very unsettling, and she had become closer to Savina and Isabel. They were quite the threesome as they made their way around the mansion.

I felt the timing was perfect for me to ask Kovak about Isabel without sounding as if I was questioning their relationship. It's one thing to be loyal to a person, but if you're going to address an issue concerning that person's lover, it would behoove you to be extremely cautious; and that's exactly what I did.

"Can I have a word with you?" I said to Kovak.

"Certainly, my son, it must be a matter of importance for you to be up so early."

"I think so, and I believe it will be of importance to you as well."

"Ah, then go ahead. Don't be nervous, you have nothing to fear."

I was still a bit hesitant before responding, "It's about, Isabel." His eyebrows instantly arched upwards as he calmly stared at me.

"Go on."

"On her trips to the town, she has been friendly with several humans, mostly young girls. She spends a lot of her time with them. I'm deeply troubled by it. As humans, her father and Mr. Buchanan were great friends, and I would see her and Benjamin quite often. She's the friendly type and her being with the humans might . . ." He calmly cut me off.

"This is of importance, I wondered at times about the few items she would return with."

"And what did she say?" I asked him mindful of how I said it.

"She mentioned that she would visit her family's farm and nightfall would catch her at times. Not that she's afraid of the dark by any means," he laughed aloud. I couldn't help but laugh as well. "She was also fascinated by her new generation of family members who knew nothing of her, and she wanted to see them."

"I see. But isn't it some distance away?" I asked.

"My son, did it take you long to get from Virginia to here?"

I quickly got his point. She visited as she said. I thought to myself. At times, I certainly felt like visiting Buchanan's Big House.

"I understand."

"Her being as friendly as you say, might be a bit troubling. How did you find this out, Salas?"

"She told me this herself."

"I see. So, it is indeed the truth. I know at times she can be a tad naive, but I will talk with her. I want you to keep an eye on that situation as well."

"I will. One more thing, she has introduced her brother to one of the girls. Benjamin introduced us. He was the one who brought it to my attention."

He took a deep breath before sitting down. He smiled, and then said, "Not a word of this should reach anyone else's ear. You and I will look into this matter."

"Yes," I replied.

"Come, let's have a drink." I often wondered if he drank any strong beverages before he was turned.

EPISODE
16

"Excuse me." It was the familiar voice of, Koshen.

"How can I help you?"

"Since the humans started their war, Kovak has put you in charge of the blood supply. Why is that?"

"What do you mean? What are you talking about?"

"Since you have been amongst us, you have been a thorn in my side. My friends are no longer with us. You have stolen my beloved. Kovak has put you in charge of everything around here. Do you also aspire to replace him?"

"Hmm, now it all makes sense, you're under the impression that I want to lead the coven. And what makes you think that? Kovak isn't going anywhere. So, what would make you think that?"

"Don't patronize me, Salas. You know exactly what I mean. I was his favorite. I was to marry, Ravina. I was held in high esteem until you came along. Now, look at what you almost did."

"And what might that be?"

"You almost had Ravina killed. You had no reason to take her into town. If I weren't there Trajar's men would have killed her."

"I loathe you. You're poisoned with hate. How dare you approach me with nothing but fabrication and lies?" I snarled at him as my fangs slowly protrude.

"It doesn't matter what you have told Kovak. You and Ravina know the truth," he snarled in return. "So, did you find out who is responsible for the death of all those humans?"

"No, have you? I could use some help."

"Find it yourself," he snapped, before leaving in a blur. I chuckled to myself as I walked to my room. This certainly was something I had to share with Ravina.

***

I sat at my desk memorizing several of the languages I had committed to memory. I studied from the books in Kovak's study. I had to retain all the information this way; I'd be prepared whenever he approached me. He would surprise me at every opportunity by speaking in any one of the languages and this I was mindful of.

After some time, I decided to take a walk. A walk that took me to where it all started. My heart was troubled, and as I made my way through the woods; there it was. I stood there in disbelief as I looked on.

106

It was the Big House. A drastic change had taken place and it was visible. There were still slaves on the land, but with the ongoing war, their workload had lessened. The few whites that I saw had to be members of the Buchanan family. They along with the blacks watched me in the distance, and as I approached, they seemed startled by my appearance and how fine I was dressed. I heard the murmurs. I now stood close enough for them to touch me.

"What it is you want nigger?" a white male yelled. I didn't respond. "Nigger, don't you hear me?"

It was only then that I realized what he was saying. I was lost in my thoughts as I stared at the slave quarters where Evelyn and my children slept. I paid attention to the old shed behind the cistern where she and I would sneak to and make love.

"What did you say?" he was quite alarmed as he stared at me with a puzzled look on his face, because of how I addressed him. The slaves were taken aback as well.

"He said what you want nigger?" another white male responded. "Don't you know you're supposed to address every white man as sir, nigger? And where did you get those fine clothes from? A nigger shouldn't be dressed like that."

"Well, I used to live here a long time ago, and now that I'm a freeman, I decided to see if anything had changed. As for your other questions, I don't have to address you as sir. I dress like this every day. You should think about dressing like this also. I bet your wife would love you even more so than she does right now." The blacks were shocked. It was written all over their faces. They couldn't believe that I had spoken to a white man in such a manner.

KARL ANTHONY

A young white male appeared out of nowhere with a rifle in his hand. It was aimed at me. I didn't flinch. I remained calm. I coldly stared at the fellow to who I was talking. He stared at the young fellow and said, "Put it away, there's no need for that."

"Are you sure?" he asked looking at me, then at the older man.

"Yes, put it away," he replied. He then turned and said to the man that I first encountered, "He's just looking. He's not a problem."

"Thank you. You have a wonderful day," I said, before turning and walking away. With the Yankees marching closer to the south, I got the sense the fellow knew that something big was coming that would change the country. My soul was pained as the memories of the Big House fell on my shoulders and buckled my knees as I kept walking. Once I was out of their sight, I took off in a blur and made my way to Ravina's chamber.

***

Kovak was in his chamber when Isabel entered. He didn't say a word. He smiled. She was surprised by his behavior.

"Why are you pondering my dear? I'm not angry at you. But isn't there something that you need to tell me?"

"You mean . . ."

"Yes, your nightly adventures," he said, cutting her off.

"I enjoy the crisp cool breeze of the night, my love. It was you who challenged me to love and accept the darkness because it's who we are. Surely, my passion and love for the daylight I do enjoy because as a human it was all I knew. But you, my love, have changed my outlook.

And although we walk amongst the humans in the day, my affection for the darkness has not quenched."

"Ah, you explained it eloquently my love. However, I'm worried about your being out late. Our enemies are vicious and cunning. Many of whom are from the Old World. My heart would be deeply pained if I were to lose my one and true love."

"I understand. I will not stay out too long."

I listened as Ravina revealed this to me. It was Savina who brought it to her attention.

"I'm worried about your sister."

"Why?"

"Because of her friendship with Isabel and Nalia."

"I see nothing wrong with it. Nalia seems to be a rather nice girl, isn't she?"

"Of course, but looks can be deceiving. Our coven is faced with enemies on all fronts and her appearance bothers me. Could she be responsible for the killings of humans?"

"Did you bring this to Kovak's attention?"

"Yes, I did."

"What was his response?"

"He said that she would remain with us indefinitely unless something else arises."

"I find nothing wrong with that."

"But what has troubled me the most is her scent."

"She does have a scent."

"Yes, she does, but when I first saw her, I didn't pick it up until later."

KARL ANTHONY

"Kovak is a smart man; he knows what he's doing."

"That he is."

As I lay in bed with Ravina, I was overwhelmed with thoughts of not only the humans, but Evelyn as well. She saw the troubled look on my face and put her arms around me. Her lips were glued to mine and as her tongue darted in and around my mouth, my urges were heightened. It was a possessive and passionate kiss, and as I reciprocated, I wrapped my arms around her neck pulling her closer and deepening the kiss as I sucked her tongue.

Her fresh womanly scent captivated my very being as I straddled her. Our vampire passion for each other consumed us as we rode each other into ecstasy. It was erotic as her supple body withstood my enlarged undead manhood. Ravina was my mysterious seductive creature. She had become my eternal and perfect mate. That night our lovemaking continued right up until dawn. It felt like the sunshine shining through the clouds after a round of torrential rainfall. It was a moment in time and for the first time in a long time, my thoughts were pure.

EPISODE
17

"Madeline, are you ok?" Benjamin whispered as he held her at arm's length, searching her face as she stood with a worried look in her eyes.

"Yes. I'm fine. But my heart is deeply troubled."

"What is wrong?"

"Do you believe in vampires?"

"Vampires?" He had a shocked look on his face. Does she know about me? He thought to himself.

"The townspeople are becoming more desperate each day, because of all the vampire killings and some have said that one of the vampires has a startling resemblance to your sister."

"That is ludicrous! Aren't I with you each day? Vampires are night creatures! That's impossible."

"I know, and this is what I told my friends. But the townspeople are plotting to kidnap her next time she's in town."

"How silly can they be? So, what have they said about me, knowing that she's my sister?"

"They didn't say."

"Can't you try and convince them that they are wrong?"

"Don't worry, they didn't say it was her for sure, remember? They said she resembled Isabel. But I will do my best along with my family."

"Thank you, my love."

As I sat there listening to Benjamin, I was in disbelief. Several things crossed my mind as he continued.

"This is grave news, and we have to bring it to Kovak's attention."

"Indeed. I spoke to my sister, and she denies being the one behind the killings."

"I see."

"What's next, Salas?"

"We will visit, Kovak."

Benjamin and I entered the main study, and there Kovak stood chatting with several of our allies. Their eyes fell upon us as we made our way across the room. Kovak quickly sensed the seriousness of our appearance and excused himself. The members of our coven had a look of alarm on their faces as well. They stopped speaking and turned and stared at the three of us. Their expressions were a combination of fear and intrigue as we left in a blur.

"What is it?" Kovak asked.

"Benjamin, explain," I said.

Kovak was visibly upset as he summoned Isabel. "Go to my chambers and remain there," he told her as she smiled at me and Benjamin.

Once she was out of our sight, Kovak summoned the Council and the Argi. "The humans are claiming that someone that resembles Isabel is responsible for the recent killings."

"What do we do now?" an elder asked.

"I will deal with Isabel. In the meantime, alert our coven of what it is the humans' plan to do."

"It is done, Kovak!" the elders said in unison.

Kovak dismissed the elders and told me and Benjamin to go to the edge of town and keep an eye on the townspeople.

***

"My sweet Isabel, is there anything that you need to share with me?"

"Why would you ask such a question, my dear, Kovak? You know how I feel about you. I'm bound to spend eternity with you, my love."

"Then why are you trying to fight me? You are no match for me?" She tried desperately to block her thoughts, but it was to no avail.

"I'm nervous. I'm afraid that I might be accused of something that I didn't do."

"If it weren't for my love for you, I would have ripped you apart. You are being dishonest. Our coven survival could be in jeopardy, because of your dishonesty. Now tell me!" he barked, his voice shaking her very being.

"It is me! I have been feeding on humans. I'm sorry."

"But why? Of all the covens ours is supplied with the highest quality of human blood."

"I can't explain why. It was instinctive. I felt it deep within me fighting, pushing, and trying to escape. And when I acted upon the urges, I felt better."

Isabel had a surprised look on her face as Kovak smiled. He understood. It was a part of the undead makeup; some of us have better control of it than others and it was obvious that Isabel didn't.

"I know your pain; it will be fine. I understand. I won't let anything happen or allow anyone to hurt you. But you must no longer go around the humans. Our covens and each other is what sustains us and that's how we have survived for thousands of years," he said, gently taking hold of her hands.

She stood before him unsure of her self-control and urges; even though he had assured her that she must remain disciplined to fight off the urges. Upon hearing this, I was relieved that he had addressed this matter. In the past, this was a problem for our coven, especially amongst the younger vampires. I had the urges, but I was unwavering and remained so.

My heart goes out to Isabel because she and I were turned the very same night and some things impeded us at times. It's an unbelievable feeling hearing a human heart beating when it reaches your ears. It's a rush that heightens all your senses and your thirst is unquenchable. It's a terrible faith being one of the undead and I have accepted it.

***

Kovak's suspicion was aroused as the killing of the humans continued. Isabel had reassured him and the Argi that she wasn't responsible for the continued killings. It was brought to my attention. I was baffled as I tried to make sense of it.

"I just don't get it. If it isn't her then who else could it be?" He observed me with wary eyes.

"Someone else is behind this, and I'm going to find out who it is."

"Yes, this is a problem. It could be any one of our enemies or even someone amongst us."

"Indeed, my son; but we have to be vigilant in our quest to get to the bottom of this."

"Do you think it's, Nalia?"

"Not at all, she hasn't been out of my sight; but you might be on to something."

"What do you mean?"

"It could be our long-lost and most formidable foe," he smiled.

"It was he who sent those killers after me and Ravina. Why did Trajar send those killers after her? What's more troubling is that I overheard Koshen asking her if she had told me her little secret."

"My son, in due time I will fill you in."

"But don't you think that now is a good time?"

He stared at me with those steely dark eyes of his, before saying, "In due time, as I said." I nodded and said I understood.

It wasn't long thereafter that an angry mob of humans, obviously frustrated, torched, burned, and killed several of our brothers and sisters.

KARL ANTHONY

We spared no one as we ravished and maimed with an unseen vengeance. It was an all-out assault on both sides. The bloodshed and fatality grew. We fought for our lives and held the humans at bay. And as time went on, they eventually succumb and fled for their lives. We were at peace with the humans once again.

I felt terrible for Benjamin; most of Madeline's family was wiped out. The family's slaves weren't spared either, or those that weren't killed fled for their lives. Madeline later moved in with several family members but was treated awful. She begged Benjamin if she could move in with him and that's when he suggested the most outlandish thing I had ever heard.

"She keeps begging me, Salas. What else can I do?"

"I feel your pain, my young friend. Love will do that to you."

"There's something out there that's bigger than us and it's not on our side."

"What do you mean?"

"Our enemies have joined together to wage war against us, and they are murdering the humans as we speak. Her life is in danger. I don't want to lose her. We were together last night, and I wanted so much to turn her, but I couldn't do it. Therefore, I seek your help."

"Does she love you as much as you love her?"

"Yes, she would do anything for me."

"Are you willing to walk away and never see her again, if she doesn't agree with what I'm about to say to you?"

"What do you mean?"

"Tell her."

"That I'm one of the undead?"

"Yes, if not, then walk away; and I mean now."

Benjamin turned his back to me as he contemplated his next move. What else could I have said or done? It was a decision that he had to make, and I wondered what kind of decision, I would have made under those dire circumstances. Turning to me, he said, "I will take your advice."

EPISODE
18

The next night . . .

"**M**adeline, we need to talk," Benjamin said to her taking her hand.
"Oh, Benji, I was worried about you. How much longer are we going to live under these conditions? I don't want to be here. I want to be with you."

"This is why I am here. I am here to take you with me, but I need to ask you something."

"Of course, ask."

"Do you love me?"

"Of course, I do. Why would you ask such a thing?"

"Because your answer will decide our future." She glared at him in a non-threatening way.

"So, what is it?"

"Remember the conversation that you and I had about my sister?"

"Yes."

"Well, she's a . . ."

"Vampire!"

"How the fuck . . ."

"I know that you are a vampire too, Benji."

"You knew all this time and never said a word about it to me?"

"I was waiting for you to tell me."

"How and when did you find out?"

"Your sister told me."

"What? She did?"

"I saw her and a female friend behind the woods and I heard screams. I should have been afraid, but I wasn't. I walked over to where the screams were coming from and there she was with her friend. I saw what they were doing, but I wasn't angry. I was angry with my neighbors and the townspeople who sought to destroy your kind. Isabel made me vow to secrecy and I never said a word to anyone. Strangely, I wanted what she and her friend had, including you. I saw her friend during the last battle with the townspeople."

"You did?"

"Yes, I did."

Benjamin was at a loss for words because he never knew that Isabel was the one killing the humans. He and I had talked about it on numerous occasions, but I never told him what I knew. This only confirmed our speculations at least mine, that she continued doing it without Kovak's knowledge. Also, the description that Madeline gave him of Isabel's friend was non-other than Savina.

"So Benji, now that I have told you all this, does it now make sense to you when I repeatedly told you that I wanted to leave and be with you?"

"Yes, it does. But what about your family, they were killed by my coven?"

"My family never liked you. I didn't care for them. I wasn't well-liked by my parents; they showed a lot more attention to my two older siblings. I want you, that is where my heart lies."

"I want you too, my love. Come." He held her in his arms. "You know, I haven't been a vampire for a long time. My sister and I, along with Salas were turned the same night. Even as a human, I never felt anything that I feel with you as a vampire. I have met my match in you, my love."

They held hands while enjoying the moonlit night. Madeline listened intently thinking how ironic it was that of all her friends she would be the one courted by a creature, a vampire, a predator that her friends had no idea existed. Her overwhelming urge to become one of the undead was startling, high drama, and tension-filled. At times, Benjamin said it was hilarious and it made him chuckle as they spoke at length.

"If we're going to be together there are some things you're going to have to learn." Madeline smiled at him.

"And what's that? I thought I learned all that I needed to know."

"Well, you need to know that whenever we kiss, I lose control. Because I know what you're working with because I felt it." She giggled.

"I don't want to hurt you and that is why I take my time. Don't forget you are still human. And you know my passion for you is overwhelmingly strong."

"Then you should do what you came here to ask me. I'm ready."

"The abyss of the undead is dark my love and vicious."

As I listened to Benjamin, I was fascinated by what he was saying. He went on to say that as he worked his way down to her neck, she shuddered. He gently caressed and nibbled his way down her smooth milky flesh; by now she was more relaxed and his protruding fangs seared into her flesh, sending searing pain through her body.

"I was surprised that she didn't scream," he revealed to me. The horrendous pain and vivid nightmares that all the undead experienced, Madeline had to experience for herself.

EPISODE
19

It had always been my intention to sit down with Isabel and explain to her the consequences of not following Kovak's orders. Yet I was angrier at Savina for taking her on a series of attacks against the humans. She should have known better. She has been by Kovak's side for hundreds of years and for her to go on these rampages with someone so young and without permission was irresponsible. It was a picturesque evening when I approached both women along with Nalia in the garden.

"Hello, ladies."

"Hi, Salas," they said in unison.

"Something was recently brought to my attention that you both were a part of. Care to expound on it?"

"About?" Savina asked.

"The killings of the humans; we all know that you two were involved. Kovak wants to know why. Isabel, didn't you tell her about your conversation with Kovak?"

"No."

"What conversation?" Savina asked.

"I don't know what Kovak is going to do or say, knowing that you were a part of this Savina, especially since you are more seasoned than Isabel. Why did you show up on the night we fought the humans? You weren't supposed to be there?"

"Who said I was there?"

"Come on now, Savina."

"Who said I was?"

"She did," I said, as Madeline appeared with Benjamin by her side.

She was surprised to see Madeline and then it dawned on her that she was turned. Isabel was excited. She couldn't control her excitement as she hugged her and Benjamin. Nalia looked on as if none of what we were discussing mattered. I returned my focus to Savina.

"So, do we have an understanding now?"

"Yes," she said, with some reluctance.

"Excuse me," Nalia said turning to Isabel. "Is that your brother?"

"Yes," Isabel said to her as the rest of us looked on trying to make sense of where this was going.

"Ladies," I interrupted. "Our coven survival is paramount and no one individual or individuals are bigger than the coven and these are Kovak's words." My eyes were on Nalia as I spoke, and although Kovak said she wasn't a threat, I still had my doubts.

KARL ANTHONY

***

During the fighting between the north and south, the slaves were freed, and although I was no longer human, I felt a sense of attachment as several emotions flowed through my very being. I was thrilled that the slaves could now live a secure life, founded on the principles of Liberty, Life, and the pursuit of Happiness. However, that was not to be the case.

After four years of bloodshed, the South surrendered, and the Civil War ended. The year was 1865. We knew the day would come, but we had become accustomed to the endless supply of blood, and like the other covens, we didn't like the outcome.

I was worried. The humans were now united and our coven like the others felt threatened. Within months of the surrender, we were at war with the humans — picking up where we left off. I was told repeatedly that since our existence, our kind has been warring with the humans and there was never a time when we had actual peace; and even when we did, it was short-lived.

I yearned for a time of peace and a world where we could live with humans without fear of each other. Kovak, Tazar, and the Argi lectured us on the history of our coven at every opportunity. They boasted about the coven's wealth, accomplishments, its conquest of the Old World; and what the coven needed to do to conquer the future. Even our enemies lived in splendor; this was something that I never could have imagined if I weren't one of the undead. I had accepted my faith and all the accolades that came with it, whether good or bad.

I was sent as an emissary on behalf of my maker to engage the other covens in unifying as one body, to prevent the humans from taking up arms against us whenever they pleased. Our problem has always been the scattered factions that used the most vicious tactics from the Old World against each other while warring with the humans. Kovak wanted us to form a permanent coalition of resistance against humans.

It was discouraging as more than sixty percent of the covens decided not to join the coalition. I tried my best to convince them of the long-term ramification it would have in the future.

"Aren't you tired of the warfare and want some kind of peace?" I asked those in attendance.

"Surely, our accomplishments speak for themselves," they carried on, totally ignoring the reality that the humans were inventing and creating a few formidable weapons to destroy our kind.

"We are not like the humans," one of them suggested. "We are the undead. We have lived for thousands of years. It doesn't matter how many weapons they invent. They are no match for us."

Sadly, they failed to see the point of my coming there. I said to them before leaving that whatever discord they have with Kovak and Tazar, our entire survival is in imminent danger and another leader will bring about some transparency to the grave and dire situation that is upon us.

"We will destroy our human enemies," several of them roared in unison.

"Let's not forget that we were once human before becoming one of the undead," I stated. There was a stirring silence. They had a grim look on their faces. I didn't say another word, as I left with Koshen, Benjamin, Ravina, and Isabel.

KARL ANTHONY

***

We were greeted by Kovak and the others upon our return to the mansion. He wanted to know if we had made any progress. I informed him of what transpired and how unwilling they were to even listen to most of what I had to say.

"It's not the message they have a problem with; it's who it came from," Kovak said to me.

"I understand. But it's common sense."

Chuckling, he said, "Ah, common sense doesn't work all the time. I knew what I was doing when I sent you there. I was hoping that they would use common sense, but again it has failed."

"Kovak, may I remind you that some of our fellow vampires do not think like many of us from the Old World," Tazar added.

"You are correct my friend. We now have a daunting task ahead of us. Those scattered factions that are always starting these senseless fights; the time has come for us to crush them. It's the only way we can stay focused on Trajar and humans. Rusk, Rant, and Tiago must be eliminated. It is their covens that the others follow."

Koshen didn't say much, but his body language and demeanor were noticeable. He had a thirst for blood and Kovak's words resonated with him. I knew he had an agenda and would at any minute turn against me, because of Ravina. Yet he always kept his thoughts private. I tried unsuccessfully on a few occasions to get a breakthrough but never could.

EPISODE
20

I was reading about the Old World when I felt the presence of someone standing by the door. "Come in," I said.

"Hi, Salas."

"How are you and what brings you here?"

"I just thought I'd stop by and see how you are doing."

"How kind of you."

"Don't you find me attractive?"

"What did you say?"

"I said, don't you find me attractive?"

"I find you attractive . . . no, no, what I mean is that you are attractive. Yeah, that's right!"

"You don't find me attractive in any other way?"

"In what way?"

"In making love to me."

"I cannot do such a thing, Ravina is my love."

"I'm aware of it, but I'm much prettier and younger."

"I think it is time that you leave my room."

"Afraid, are you? Well?"

"It's time for you to leave!" I said. I grabbed hold of her and in a blur; I escorted her from my room.

"You know you can't resist my charm," she giggled, walking away.

"Don't flatter yourself." I felt a sudden wind and turned around just in time to see Koshen in the hallway.

"You're after her as well? The one you stole from me isn't, enough? Oh, I get it; you just want all the women around here, don't you?"

"What do you want?" I snapped at him.

"Listen, I had no intention of coming here. I only came at the urging of your maker. He wants you to meet him with the others in the main quarters. Be on time and dress for the occasion. Oh, Nalia will be there," he said, with a sinister smile.

Occasion? I thought to myself. Within minutes, I was dressed in the finest tailored suit. I splashed on one of the fragrances that Ravina had given me. I was quite dapper as I made my way down the hall. I heard what sounded like a celebration. Ravina greeted me as I entered the regal room, which was decorated with all the splendor of a grand gala. As Ravina and I made our way through the crowded room, I was relieved to see Kovak. I wanted to know what brought about this festive occasion. Ravina didn't know either, like me, she was summoned as were the others.

"What's the occasion?" I asked Kovak. With him were Isabel, Tazar, the Council, and the Argi. Koshen and Nalia stood a few feet away drinking and laughing.

"We are here to welcome Benjamin's new love, Madeline. It was my idea. What do you think?"

"It's a great idea."

"I knew you would agree. Let us welcome them."

We greeted them with open arms, affection, and love. This was our coven. We were a family. This was our moment, and we relished every minute of it. We were the undead, and at that moment, we were one voice, one nation; a group of vampires that welcomed another into our midst. Benjamin was thrilled. He was speechless as he stood there alongside Madeline, who had a flustered look on her face. But as the celebration continued her uneasiness gave way to one of jubilation.

As I expected, Nalia approached me as soon as Ravina left my side. What I didn't know was that Ravina had noticed her eyeing me and stood off to the side watching the whole thing unfold.

"What is it now, Nalia?" I asked. She was trying her best to block her thoughts from me, but she was still young and naïve. She hadn't mastered all the intricacies of how to fully do so.

"Would you like to dance?"

"Sure," I said.

I knew her motives and I held her in a manner that made her upset. I couldn't help but smile to myself. I must admit, she was a great dancer.

At the end of the dance, I respectfully thanked her. She wasn't pleased, as she frowned, sucked her teeth, and walked away.

"She has a crush on you, my love," Ravina said, as I took her in my arms and began dancing.

"How do you know this? Did you read her thoughts?"

"No, there wasn't a need for that, I'm a woman."

"Indeed, you are," I chuckled, as we waltz to the classically trained piano playing of Tazar. "There remain some things which are troubling."

"You mean with Nalia?"

"Yes."

"At times, I have my doubts about her as well; so yes, I can understand."

"Nothing has happened of late other than our continuous wars with the humans and I haven't seen anything else for that matter. Have you?"

"No, but what do you mean?"

"You should know, you have been with Kovak for most of your life and you have seen a lot during that time."

"I have. I understand now. But do you think she's up to something?"

"It's hard to say. She hasn't given us anything, nothing."

"Right. We would destroy her if she did. She must know this. She has to know that some in our coven are from the Old World and would be able to read her thoughts easily. I was able to do so within minutes."

"So that's how you knew she had a crush on me, huh?"

Giggling, she said, "Partially, yes, but it's more of a woman's intuition."

"I understand. Let's enjoy the night, but certainly not lose sight of our coven's survival and those who will do anything to destroy us."

"Certainly!"

"What do you think of Benjamin and Madeline?"

"They make a nice couple, but a number of the girls were upset that he chose a human, one that he turned."

"But weren't we all humans once upon a time? I just don't get it."

"I'm just telling you what the girls have been saying," she laughed.

"Okay! Have you met her?"

"I did, and she seems like a nice person."

"A nice vampire, huh?" we couldn't help but laugh.

Moments later, Benjamin said a few words and graciously thanked Kovak for his hospitality. Madeline also said a few words, before settling down with Isabel and the other girls.

EPISODE
21

One month later, Kovak's words came to fruition as our coven clashed with Rusk, Rant, and Tiago's covens, in the town of Shrewsbury. The town's people stayed clear of the woods. It was a bloody period. The carnage was brutal and gory. I surprised Rusk as he tried to attack Benjamin from the shadows. In a blur, I side-stepped him and snapped his neck. I was quickly pinned down by two of their goons, but Kovak with one swing of his sword tore their heads from their bodies. I viciously began snapping their necks, as I made my way through the mob of hissing vampires.

What none of us knew was that both Rusk and Tiago had pledged their allegiance to Rant. They had recruited several fugitive vampires to fight alongside them. They traveled from as far away as North Carolina.

They scaled mountains and traveled through creeks and forests only to succumb to the wrath of Kovak, the Great Vampire King. They fought with their traditional swords and waged a fierce battle, but it was all for nothing.

According to Kovak, Rant had double-crossed Rusk and Tiago and they had gone their separate ways years earlier. For 500 years no one heard anything about them. It wasn't until our battles on the North American continent did the three of them surfaced. It was great knowing their history, but on this day, it was their time to meet their maker, Hell; and that is exactly where we send them.

As the last of our enemies fled, I noticed Koshen and Nalia. I was shocked. Kovak had to have seen them, I said to myself — when in a blur, he snatched Koshen by the neck and shrieked a loud hiss that reverberated so loud that the fleeing group panicked.

"Why did you bring her here?" Kovak roared. "Didn't I tell you to remain at the mansion with her and the others? Didn't I?"

"She was persistent. She wanted to fight. I explained . . ."

"Say no more! I will deal with this upon our return to the mansion. Come, let us go."

No sooner than we arrived at the mansion, Koshen was called to Kovak's private library. He was angry as he entered, and my being there only made matters worse. Tazar was also there, but he wasn't a problem.

"How dare you go against my instructions?" Kovak barked at him.

"She begged me. I told her what you said."

"So, she's now telling you what to do? Are you out of your fucking mind?"

"I'm sorry. I promise it will never happen again."

133

"Ever since you began fucking her, you have been doing a lot of silly things that are uncalled for," Tazar added.

I was beside myself. It had crossed my mind that they were sleeping together. But I never actually thought that he would.

"Is that it?" Kovak asked him."

"No, Kovak. I apologize. It wasn't sound judgment on my part, and it won't happen again."

"Where is she?"

"She's in the library."

"Summon her."

We were talking when she entered. "This is beautiful," she said, staring at the vast library. It was off-limits to her.

"Nalia!" Kovak said. "You are not allowed in combat unless I give the order. Do you hear me?"

She had a frightened look on her face. "I didn't know. I'm sorry. I felt it was my duty to fight alongside my new coven, my family. Please forgive me."

"Ah, your apology is accepted."

"Thank you, Kovak," Koshen added, as they left us alone.

"Strange little thing, isn't she?" Tazar said.

"Indeed," I responded. "I never knew they were a couple. Isn't she too young for him?"

Both men laughed, before Kovak said, "We are vampires. We are the undead. Our love is unlike humans. But I can assure you, she is of age." They laughed aloud. I couldn't help but join them.

***

That night we drank the finest blood in celebration of our victory. After some time, Tazar left our presence and that's when I brought up Veech and Zan.

"What about them?" Kovak asked.

"You have been a father to me, and I just wanted to know if you were the one who killed them." I feared he would be angry at me for asking such a question, but instead, his response surprised me.

"You are my son, Salas, and I will be honest with you. No, it wasn't me or Tazar. Tana was special to me. I miss her dearly. She meant everything to me and their lack of judgment, betrayal, or whatever it was, that drove them to act and respond the way they did, led to her death. It pains me deeply, knowing that she is no longer here."

"I understand. I was just troubled by it that's all. As I said before, Benjamin thought he heard strange noises and he thought I should know. Please don't be angry at him for telling me this."

"Quite the contrary my son, I think Benjamin is a fine young man. I hold him in high esteem. You have taught him well. However, someone amongst us carried it out."

"Thank you for your kind words. But who could that someone be?" I was about to mention Koshen's name when he smiled.

"I know what you're thinking. But it could have been a woman as well. It could be anyone, but I assure you that I will find out who did it."

"I agree with you, it could be anyone."

"Trajar is the cause of me losing my Tana, and I will not rest until he's destroyed."

"I will stand by your side my King and I will fight to the death alongside you."

"My son, I know you will and that is why I chose you. I see a lot of myself in you as a young man. Our coven needs warriors like you and Benjamin. Tazar and I have been here for hundreds of years and perhaps one day you can take the reign of our coven."

"Those are kind words. I'm humbled."

"Ah, it's alright my son. It's alright. So there, Veech and Zan, I will not miss, because I lost my Tana; but I promise you, if there's one amongst us that has done this, he or she will have to explain themselves," he finished up.

"I agree. It's always wonderful to talk to you. But I shall now excuse myself for the night."

Smiling, he said, "I think that would be a most wonderful idea."

"Why are you smiling?"

"My sweet Isabel has arrived."

"Say no more," I smiled, and as I made my way out of the library, there she stood. She smiled and waved at me.

***

As I headed to my room, I was approached by Koshen. I felt sorry for him because of how Kovak admonished him in front of us. He was apologetic and tried to explain himself to me. I made it clear to him that I understood how a girl as beautiful as Nalia can take advantage of their situation.

"I know I have been a thorn in your side at times, but I want you to know that I do respect you."

"I appreciate your thoughts and I'm humbled."

"I just wanted you to know that I'm not your enemy. Kovak is our King, and we are brothers from the same coven."

"I understand."

"You know, I was once the most ferocious young vampire in our coven. I did a lot of terrible things that I'm not proud of. It was back in the Old Country. I killed any and everything that threatened our coven. I was built in the image of my maker, and I killed with reckless abandonment. I wanted the same kind of love from Kovak that he showed Savina, Ravina, and Tana. It was I who nursed Ravina back to health when she was hurt by Trajar. It was my blood that kept her alive when we were trapped."

"Trapped?"

"Yes."

"What happened?"

"I'll let Kovak give you all the relevant details. What I can tell you is that Trajar tried to destroy her. And she and I fought valiantly against him and his minions. How we survived, I don't have an answer for it, but I have always wanted to please, Kovak. I remember everything as if it were yesterday. The pain and heartbreak I felt during that period were unbearable."

"I can assure you that Kovak does love you. He talks glowingly of you."

"He does?" He seemed surprised. Although Kovak would get angry at him at times, not once did I ever get the impression that he didn't care for him. "That is wonderful to know. I aspire to be like him one day, King of the Vampires."

KARL ANTHONY

I listened as he continued talking. A lot of what he said was painful, but I explained to him that he had my full support. As I lay in bed that night, I kept thinking about Trajar, Ravina, and Kovak. I had to find a way to ask Kovak without prying into his private affairs. I considered it a top priority because she was now a part of my life.

EPISODE
22

I was in town early one afternoon when my senses alerted me to the hissing of the undead. Although the tension between us and the humans had lessened some, there was still fear on both sides. We didn't know who the vampire killers were, and they couldn't tell who a vampire was. Every stranger was scrutinized and there were instances where they were killed innocently for being one of the undead. As the hissing became louder, I picked up on the smell, it was from our coven. I waited to see who it was.

"Hello, Salas."

"Hi, Savina! Hi, Nalia! What bring you ladies to town?"

"Nothing special, it's a lovely day, so we decided to enjoy the weather. Remember, it wasn't too long ago that I wasn't able to walk in the sun," Savina said.

"I understand."

"Nalia and I came to pick up a few items."

"Yes, Salas, wanting for anything?" Nalia teased.

"Thank you, but I am fine."

"Well, Nalia and I will see you back at the mansion." Savina was about to walk away.

"Wait!" I called out to her.

"What is it?"

"Things are going great with the humans, please do not . . ."

"Salas, I know."

"Kovak warned you once before and I don't think he would be pleased if you were to get into an unfortunate situation."

"I won't."

***

The next day . . .

"How dare you say such things to me in front of Nalia?" an enraged Savina said, approaching me.

"What are you talking about?"

"Yesterday!"

"Oh, let me make this clear to you — you are not and will not jeopardize our coven because of your selfish ways. Kovak has told you this on several occasions and you behave as if you're only concerned about yourself."

"I have been with Kovak for several hundred years,' way before your ass was ever thought of, and I will not let you talk to me anyway that you please. Where you were when our women were attacked, kidnapped, stripped, and sold to other covens across the Old World? Where you were when our warriors were captured, castrated, and had to live as eunuchs and became the laughingstock of the other covens? Where, Salas?"

"I don't give a damn how long you have been by Kovak's side. And what took place then had no bearing on me because I wasn't there. I'm here now and I'm telling you that our coven is more important than any selfish individual. It was you along with Isabel that attacked the humans when we were trying to keep the peace. You should have known better then because according to you, you have been with Kovak for several years. Yet you kept Nalia a secret and convinced Isabel to go along with it. Now if I may, doesn't that sound selfish to you?"

"You are not my maker!" she screamed at me, her fangs protruding. I accepted her challenge when I suddenly caught Ravina's scent.

"This is uncalled for!" she said aloud. "Savina, go!"

"This is not over, Salas!" she said, walking away. In a blur, I was in her face. I hissed and protruded my fangs before calming down.

"Salas let her go." I did as Ravina asked. Savina was enraged; her deep eyes were filled with rage as she disappeared from our site.

"What happened?" Ravina asked. I explained to her what happened.

"She's my sister, but she's been out of control lately, and I'm worried. I know Kovak will not put up with it much longer."

"When she calms down, she'll see that what I said makes a lot of sense."

As we chatted, Kovak's hissing reverberated throughout the mansion. This was a serious matter and one which had me worried. Normally, a hiss of this kind usually is a call to battle.

There was a nervous look on everyone's face when I got to the main library. Kovak, Tazar, the Council, and the Argi were seated with a look of great concern on their faces. I too had a worried look on my face upon seeing theirs.

"My children," Kovak started, "we have news of Trajar's return and he's not alone. He has brought with him a vast number of fugitive vampires and an unknown number of fighters from the Old World to make war. The time has come for us to be vigilant and steadfast as our brothers and sisters' keepers. How long it will take before he reaches these shores we don't know. What we do know is that he has made it known that he's looking forward to his return and our destruction."

Our hisses reverberated loudly as the enormity and impact of Kovak's words angered us. We were ready for battle. At that moment nothing else mattered. Trajar had been our nemesis as far back as Kovak and Tazar can recall and a thorn in our sides.

"We are ready for battle!" the coven yelled. "Trajar will be destroyed!"

"Ah, my children," Kovak smiled. "Koshen, Salas, and Benjamin, make your way up here. Come!" he called out, as the others roared.

Later that evening . . .

"Kovak, this is serious," I said to him and Tazar.

"I know my son, but we will not falter. When Trajar arrives, we will be prepared. We will leave no stones unturned. His reputation is that of a maverick, but this time I promise you, he will meet his maker and all of Vampiredom including the Old and New World will be rid of him."

"I'm ready to fight."

"We know this. Kovak and I have witnessed your bravery," Tazar added.

"I'm humbled."

"Think nothing of it. You have shown your worth and our coven has been stronger since you have been here."

"I'm grateful. But what do we do in the meantime? Do we sit back and await him?"

"No, we continue doing the things we have," Kovak said.

"Fine!"

"Now, what is it that you wanted to ask me that was so important?"

"I had a situation with Savina."

"What was it?"

"I saw her in town with Nalia and I simply told her not to get into anything with the humans and she became angry with me. She later confronted me, and if it weren't for Ravina, we would have ended up in a fight. She warned me that it wasn't over. I just wanted to bring it to your attention."

"Hmm, I will talk to her."

"Thank you, how is Nalia coming along?"

"Other than her shenanigans with Koshen, she's been fine."

"I don't think she wants to go back to her coven or wherever it is that she came from."

"It seems that way, and I don't have a problem with it. As I told you before, her scent is not of our enemies. She's young, but at times I wonder about her, like you."

"Have you asked her about herself or where she's from?"

"Yes. She spoke of her human family as if she were happy that she was one of the undead. Her family was accomplished and wealthy. She's the daughter of Baron Costica of Tulcea from the Old Country."

"I see. Did she say who her maker was?"

"She doesn't. It was dark. But many of her family members were turned. They lived together and she never questioned anything."

"This is incredible, Kovak!"

"Indeed, my son. She has her moments when she tells me things. I don't question her much because I know what I'm doing."

"I trust your judgment."

"Ah, that is great news," he said, laughing. "And how are things with you and Ravina?"

"She's been the world to me."

"You still think of your human wife, my son?"

"At times I do. A while back I visited the Big House and it brought back lots of memories. So yes, at times I do."

"I understand."

EPISODE

23

Kovak and I were taking one of his daily walks. He found it very
relaxing. And I must say, I felt the same. We spoke at length,
discussing some of the great philosophers. He had great admiration for
these men. I kidded him that their frailty could be questioned. To which,
he responded, "Even the undead frailty can be questioned. Don't you
think?" He smiled at me, and I could only nod in agreement. We weren't
back at the mansion long when he asked me to accompany him to a
section that was unfamiliar to me. We followed a pathway that led to an
underground dungeon. There we came upon a huge steel door. It was
operated by an old male vampire. He whispered something in Kovak's
ear. As the door slowly opened, inside were Tazar and a member of the
Council, and Argi. They greeted me. The place was well lit.

"Come," Kovak said. I followed closely behind.

I was astonished. My knees buckled at what I saw. I stood there breathless. There in front of me was a great vault of gold currencies, paper monies, rubies, diamonds, sapphires, and some of the most precious gems in the world, standing guard were six male and female guards. They were called the Aryaa, which when translated means the Keeper of the Kingdom.

"What is the matter, Salas?"

"I'm speechless."

"Speechless?"

"Yes, I have never seen anything like this. Why have you shown me this?"

"Because you are the Protector of our Coven, come." A few feet away stood an odd shape looking door, Tazar pulled a lever and an old, covered manuscript appeared. He then handed me a bright torch. I want you to read this particular part now," Kovak said. "As of today, you are given access to read this manuscript."

"My King, my maker, I'm overwhelmed. Your kindness and confidence in me are greatly appreciated."

I began reading. Kovak Belododia was the second King of our coven called the Vladzann. Tazar was the Prince of Darkness and the Protector of the King. Our first King ruled Vampiredom before there was a Great Nile, Mesopotamia, and Night Lands. Humans, sorcery, treachery, betrayal, nor our passion for our women, or thousands of years in chains should and never hamper our way of life. We are the Undead. We Bleed for Our Coven. We Die Today. We will Reign

Supreme. Our Survival is predicated on our will to Exist. APTISSIMUS QUISQUE TANTUM SUPEREST! Means, Only the Fittest Survive.

"The meaning is written in Latin, Kovak."

"It is my son."

"Why? We existed before the Nile and other great civilizations?"

"Indeed, but if you read closely, you will see that various languages were used from what you have read so far."

"Yes, I see that, but I thought a word with such force and meaning for our coven would have been written in another language."

"Ah, I like your sense of awareness, but as you read on you will see that each group of Argi's over the years have written in different languages. Some were destroyed before completing their thoughts and others picked up from where they left off and wrote in their tongue, my son."

"Hmm, I see."

"Only the Argi can write in this tablet other than myself and Tazar. Perhaps one day you will get that opportunity."

"I am humbled, once again."

"What do you think now?"

"This is fascinating. I will take advantage of your generous offer."

"It's not a generous offer my son, you were chosen."

"Chosen?"

"Yes."

"By whom?"

"Us. All of us."

Even the rigid-looking guards had a smile on their faces. I graciously accepted my faith. A circle was formed, and I drank the blood of theirs and they drank the blood of mine. It was a ritual of acceptance and accepting that which I was chosen for. It was a symbolic act that only a few from the coven would ever see. If I ever had any doubts about my role as one of the undead, it was now in the past. On that night, surrounded by that small group, I became a full-fledged member of the Vladzann coven.

EPISODE
24

"Do you have a problem with Salas?" Kovak asked Savina.

"What do you mean?"

"He told me about your recent encounter."

"Oh, he is not my maker, you are, and I didn't appreciate how he spoke to me in front of Nalia."

"Did he disrespect you?"

"Yes, he did."

"How so?"

"He said some things which I thought was unnecessary and uncalled for."

"You mean telling you to stay away from humans? They were my orders. Is that a problem? Your decision-making of late hasn't been what I would call sensible. I don't know what is going on, but I'm hopeful that you will come around."

"What do you mean by come around?"

"You know exactly what I mean. You and your sister have been with me for many years, and I will not apologize for having you both close to my heart . . ."

"Your heart? Kovak, I have loved you ever since and you threw me to the side for Isabel. What did I do to deserve such treatment? The coven now looks at me as if something is wrong with me. How could you betray me?"

"Betray you? I'm Kovak — King of Vampiredom, I do as I please. How dare you question my motives and decisions? This is not about you; it has everything to do with me. Indeed, I do love you, but you will not be my Queen. I'm your maker and I'm telling you from this day on, that Salas speaks for me."

"You are getting soft, huh? You have never said such words before and now this newcomer to our coven is held in high esteem that he now speaks for the great, Kovak?"

"Listen," he said, snatching her by the face. "Don't you fuck with me; do you understand me? My words are final!"

As I sat there with Benjamin listening to Isabel, I feared that Savina might snap at any moment. She was angry at Isabel for replacing her as Kovak's new love, yet she befriended her and convinced her to attack the humans.

"What else did Kovak say if anything?" I asked.

"He said she stormed out of his library," Isabel said.

"I don't understand her," Benjamin added. "Why is she behaving like this?"

"I guess she felt Kovak betrayed her."

"Salas, how could she think this knowing that he's, her maker?"

"It's obvious to me that she wants to be Queen." Laughing, I added, "Are you ready to become our Queen, Isabel?"

She smiled and said, "That is a decision that I have left to Kovak."

"That's a wonderful answer," I said.

"I know," she giggled, leaving me and Benjamin alone.

I told Benjamin about my initiation and all that I saw and heard. He was fascinated by our history and wanted to know a lot more. I told him that I would share these things with him. He was deeply grateful.

***

My mind was reeling back and forth as I surveyed the main living quarters and the faces of my brothers and sisters. The sound of music reverberated throughout the halls. Everyone was enjoying themselves. Other than the threat of Trajar, we were at ease with everything else that was happening. The music was up-tempo and as Tazar joined the other musicians, a group of our shapely female members began to entertain us. They sexily danced for us, gyrating in their revealing costumes. It was a grand moment as we drank the finest blood and enjoyed the non-stop gyration and gestures of the women.

Moments later, our celebration ended abruptly, when the screams from two of Savina's friends reverberated throughout the living room. Several of us made our way to where the screams were coming from.

KARL ANTHONY

Curled up on the bed was the lifeless body of Madeline. Her body was slowly deteriorating. Blood was everywhere. It was evident that she had put up a fight.

I felt terrible for Benjamin. He was in a daze. Isabel did her best to comfort him. Kovak was visibly upset. He didn't say much, and neither did Tazar. Ravina and Nalia and several others immediately went after the culprit as soon as they got there, but they were unsuccessful. I immediately looked around for Koshen, but he was amongst the crowd. Savina was nowhere to be found. Savina? Why would she do something like this? I thought. My suspicion was heightened as I search the faces of our members. Whatever remained of Madeline was removed from the mansion. She wanted so much to be one of the undead and to be with Benjamin. I was angry.

***

The next day . . .

Benjamin and I were in town when the stench of our enemies overpowered us. We were prepared for a fight, but instead, our two approaching enemies wanted to talk. The female who seemed to be in charge was none other than my lady love, Febra. I was troubled by her sudden appearance, but at the same time, I was glad to see her.

"Salas," she said, "it's been some time since I last saw you. How have you been?"

"Yes, it's been some time, and what is this about?"

"Why so touchy, my friend? I come in peace, didn't we, Gilron?"

"Indeed," he answered.

"Who is your handsome friend, Salas?"

"My name is Benjamin," he said to her before I could respond."

"Such a new name, but I love it," she giggled.

"What is it, Febra?"

"It's about Veech and Zan."

"What about them?"

"It's funny that I know who killed them and you and the Great Kovak don't," she said, mockingly.

"What do you mean? Who killed them?"

"It was someone from your coven and we know who it is."

"Is that so?"

"Yes, we do, isn't that right, Gilron?"

"Yes, mistress!"

"Who is it? I have no time for the games." She approached me and whispered in my ears.

"It was Koshen! He killed them."

"Come," I said, taking her to the side.

"How could he? They were his friends."

"Sure, they were, but they were expendable."

"Okay, let's say I believe you. But how do you know all this?"

"In three days, meet me at the place where we first met. Don't forget."

"I will be there."

"You have a wonderful rest of the day, Benjamin," she called, walking away from me, "perhaps, I'll see you again, handsome?"

"Huh? Sure," he replied.

"Come now, Benjamin," I said, as they disappeared from our sight.

"She is beautiful. Who is she?" he asked.

"We met several years ago. I was getting used to being one of the undead and I came to town and there she was. She said hi to me and I returned the favor. But she kept following me."

"Didn't you pick up her scent?"

"I'll be honest with you, back then I couldn't tell the difference between a vampire's scent and dog shit." Benjamin roared in laughter. I couldn't help but join him.

"So, what happened next?"

"I was scared that she might have figured out that I was one of the undead and warn the town's people. I fled. I was scared. She kept following me. Suddenly, I had an insatiable hunger. I thought she would make an appetizing meal. But she was thinking the same thing as she approached me. She was one of the undead. She attacked me."

"Are you fucking serious?"

"Indeed, I am. We were by the northern end of town not too far from where the sea merchants drank, and the prostitutes worked."

"So, what happened next?"

"She couldn't believe how strong I was. She stopped when I overpowered her. Although I was young, I was powerful."

"Kovak has said that about you many times." We both laughed.

"She said I was young and that she knew I was a vampire all along, but she thought I was handsome."

"The same thing she just said about me, huh?" We began laughing once again.

"She made love to me that very night."

"Really?"

"Yes, she did. But I have something a bit more interesting to tell you."

"And what is that? What could be more interesting than you fucking her?" he laughed.

Laughing, I said, "She said Koshen was the one responsible for Veech and Zan's death."

"She told you that?" The laughter suddenly stopped.

"Yes, and when I asked her how she knows this, she said she would meet in three days and tell me."

"Do you trust her? Do you want me to come with you?"

"I will be fine. I can handle her and her friend."

"If you need me, I'm here for you."

"Thanks. That damn Koshen, I never trusted him."

"Me neither, but if it was his doing, what is he trying to prove?"

"That is the question and after all that Kovak has done for him it would be a shame if he was behind it."

"The night my Madeline was killed, I was looking to see if he was with the rest of us, and he was."

"I did also. He's been holding a grudge against me, and you since we arrived at the mansion."

"But why, Salas?"

"He believes our being at the mansion has hurt his relationship with Kovak?"

"But he's been with Kovak for hundreds of years. He thinks Kovak would give up on him because of us?"

"Pretty much! That's how he feels."

KARL ANTHONY

"I swear Salas if he has anything to do with my Madeline's death, I will destroy him."

"Hmm, we will get to the bottom of this."

Upon our return to the mansion, I explained in detail to Kovak and Tazar what Febra told me.

"If this is so, then I will deal with him," Kovak stated. "For now, let's keep this between us."

EPISODE
25

I showed up as planned, but Febra was nowhere to be found. It was a tense moment as I waited. I was prepared for battle. Why would she do this? I thought to myself. Suddenly, there was a rustle in the nearby woods. I moved closer to my intended target as I awaited its appearance. I saw a shadowy figure, and, in a flash, I pounced upon it.

"Salas, it's me. It's me, Gilron!"

"Gilron? Where is, Febra?"

"I'm here, Salas." She appeared with a smile.

"I thought you weren't going to show up. And why was Gilron creeping around?"

"Salas, we have enemies as you do. We have to be careful, plus not all of your friends like me."

"I guess I can say the same thing too, can't I?"

"Sure, you can."

"Now, where do we begin?"

"Gilron, leave us."

"Are you sure, mistress?"

"Yes; Salas is here to protect me."

"I will return in an hour or two."

"Sure!" He then took off in the night.

"Now, how did this come about?"

"As you know my coven and the Xeras have been enemies for thousands of years. But it was their new leader who I must thank for what transpired next."

"What do you mean?"

"The young girl, Nalia . . ."

"Nalia?" I said in shock, this was a bombshell. How did she know about her?

"Isn't she with your coven?"

"Yes, go on."

"She was sent by the enemies of Xeras and Trajar to infiltrate your coven and kill Kovak and destroy every one of you. She wasn't doing it on her own. She was forced to do so."

"Forced, how?"

"Trajar goons on his orders have kidnapped and chained some of her family members."

"So, which of the two covens is she a part of?"

"Neither."

"Neither?"

"Yes, I came upon her many years ago, bleeding along with her siblings and other family members. They were quite wealthy. I dare say they were one of the most influential families from the Old Country. I thought the others wouldn't make it and so I took her with me. I asked her who her maker was . . ."

"Did she recall?"

"She couldn't. She stayed with me for a while, but at the outset of the battle between us and some of the fragmented members of the Xeras, I lost her, never to see her again. It was only after my involvement with Kannis, one of the Xeras, did I find out about her."

"So, you began sleeping with the enemy? Is that, right?"

Smiling, she said, "I am who I am, Salas."

"So, what happened next?"

"Some of Trajar's men took her and ravished her. I swear; I'm going to make them pay dearly for what they did to her. They found her siblings and the others and forced her into her present situation. Salas, she's still a child. She isn't as powerful as you and me, and some of the others. This is where the story picks up, Koshen, the beloved of Kovak . . ."

"The beloved of Kovak?"

"Yes, that's how he was referred to in the Old Country. We all knew he was a favorite of Kovak."

"Hmm, continue my dearest friend."

"Now, I'm your dearest friend?" she giggled. "Koshen was lured by Trajar himself and the promise of becoming King of your coven once Kovak is killed. He orchestrated the murder of Veech and Zan because they knew too much. He wanted to take control of the coven on his own, but he realized it would be an arduous task. Veech and Zan somehow got hold of the plot to kill Kovak, but by then it was too late."

"What do you mean, by too late? Kovak is still amongst us."

"Yes, but I'm not talking about him. I'm talking about Tana. They were the ones who killed her. They wouldn't have done so according to Kannis if they knew what Koshen was plotting."

"I see."

"Fearing they might tell Kovak, he and an accomplice killed them."

"Who is the accomplice?"

"Kannis says he wouldn't say."

"Hmm."

"Don't say anything, other than take heed to the fact that it's your presence that has thrown everything in a tailspin."

"What do you mean?"

"Koshen is worried about your loyalty to Kovak and the coven. So, beware of him."

"Hmm," I smiled.

"Another thing, it's only because of how I still feel about you, that I'm sharing this with you."

"But you are content with the men in your life now, aren't you?"

"I am, but I haven't felt anything like yours since."

"Really?"

"Yes. Your friend Benjamin is handsome."

"No, he's just getting over the loss of his first love. You would tear him apart."

"Poor, baby! So, you're saying he's vulnerable, Salas?"

"No, I'm saying that he's still mourning."

"Mourning? A vampire, mourning? Are you kidding me? So, what about you, Salas, is there anyone?"

"Yes, there is someone."

"Hmm, I can wait. My eternity will be yours," she laughed aloud. In an instant, she was in my face, smiling and snarling at me. It was very erotic.

"I will keep that in mind," I said, as Gilron showed up. "I thank you for sharing this with me. I will always be in your debt."

"Sure, my love, and I will keep you to your words. Whenever you need me, I'm only but a short distance away. Salas, don't you ever forget that we share the same enemies. Oh, say hi to Kovak for me."

With those last words, she and Gilron disappeared into the night. I was baffled when she brought up Kovak's name. I had mentioned her name several times, but he never reacted as if he knew who I was talking about. Still, I wasn't going to let that take precedence over the betrayals, murders, and plots to assassinate him. There was so much to share with him and Tazar.

EPISODE
26

I noticed that Koshen wasn't with the others when I entered the mansion. I asked Benjamin if he had seen him or knew his whereabouts, and his answer was no. I hurriedly made my way with Benjamin by my side. Kovak saw the look on my face and immediately knew that I had terrible news. I told Benjamin that I would meet with him later. Kovak then gestured for me to follow him. He and I met up with Tazar and headed to his private library.

"Before you share with us the unfortunate news that you bring, I have something to share with you."

"What is it?"

"Koshen and Savina are missing, no one has seen them, and we know nothing of their whereabouts," I yelled out a hiss, which caught them by surprise.

"What's wrong? Share with us." I explained everything to both men. They were angry. The alarm was sounded, and everyone assembled in the main library.

Kovak began speaking, "Today, I was given some regrettable and terrible news. Koshen has betrayed us. Savina has been missing and I'm assuming they are together. They have jeopardized our family for others and have plotted against us with our sworn enemies. Bring them to me alive. What Koshen has done is the greatest betrayal. It goes against everything that we stand for. We ruled before there was a Great Nile, Mesopotamia, and the Night Lands." The crowd let out a great roar. "We are the Undead. We will Reign Supreme. Our Survival is predicated on our will to Exist. APTISSIMUS QUISQUE TANTUM SUPEREST, NUMAI CEL MAI TARE SUPRAVIETUIESTE."

They let out another great roar and began shouting, "Kovak, Kovak," and "Aptissimus Quisque Tantum Superest, Numai Cel Mai Tare Supravietuieste," repeatedly.

In the latter part of what Kovak said; he did so in his native tongue. I had never heard him use it before, so I was quite surprised. I wanted to hear more but now was not the time. I would wait until things were back to normal.

Several of our bravest fighters did as told, and went searching for them. Throughout Kovak's speech, Ravina and I kept eye contact and I could tell she was disheartened. I tried reading her thoughts, but she wouldn't allow it. At the end of the speech, I told her to meet me in the garden, to which she agreed.

Nalia didn't show much emotion during the speech. Something was startling about her body language and demeanor. She had to know that her life was in danger. It seemed as if she was awaiting her faith.

"Bring me, Nalia," Kovak said to Benjamin. He did as he said. There was a fearlessness about her, as she began telling Kovak of Trajar and Koshen's diabolical plan.

"Everything that Salas has said is true, my King," she said. She had never addressed Kovak in this manner before. Was she trying to fool us? What was this all about? "I have never had a place to call home since I was turned. I don't even know who my maker is. I don't know if it was a male or female. I can't say, but what I do know is that upon my arrival here, I felt welcome. And although my siblings and other family members are facing their doom, I wanted to be amongst you. I thought by trying to persuade Salas to take me, I would be accepted. I failed miserably at that. At the same time, Koshen was pursuing me, and I gave in. Yes, he was the one who told me that he and Savina were hired killers and that you, Kovak, authorized it."

"Continue, my child."

"He said you have ruled far too long and that he wasn't going to stand by, and watch Salas become the new leader. It was he who murdered Madeline along with Savina. I was sent here to harm and destroy a coven that wasn't anything like I was told. I apologize to you and the others, my King. I wish to remain amongst you and for you to help free my family from the wretched clutches of that vile and evil,

Trajar. But if you do not grant me this favor and expel me from amongst you, if possible, could you help me to return to the Old Country?"

It was a tense moment as we waited to hear what Kovak, Tazar, and the Argi had to say. I felt her pain, and I reminded Kovak that Febra's account of things supported all that she said.

"You can remain amongst us, and we will rid this world of Trajar and his goons. I will do my best to find your maker. Come, we have lots to do."

***

There were still some amongst us who had their suspicion, and rightfully so, but Nalia was being honest. Our coven had been battling for some time and had never known peace. So, I understood how they felt. Kovak and I continued talking after the others left. I wanted to know why he didn't tell me about, Febra. When I brought up her name, he let out a hearty laugh and so did Tazar. An uneasy smile was etched on my face, as I awaited his response.

"You notice that I never said anything when you first brought up her name," Kovak said, turning in Tazar's direction.

"And why was that?"

"Ask, Tazar."

"Tazar?"

"Yes, my son."

He had a sheepish grin on his face. "My boy," he said, "she's my daughter."

"Your daughter?" I couldn't believe what I was hearing.

165

"Yes, my daughter."

"So why is she not with us?"

"She chose to be with her mother's coven and hasn't spoken to me in almost a thousand years. She talks of her uncle, but not of me. I know she will come around one day. I believe so."

"Trajar and the followers of the Xeras are her enemies. She told me so. We have to help her."

"My dear boy, Febra is a fierce warrior. She knows how to take care of herself. She's been around longer than most vampires. She will be fine, but if she does need help, we will stand with her. Even though she will say no if it's offered."

"Why that look?" Kovak asked.

"It's just that . . ."

"That you care about her?"

"I do. She's a friend."

"She's my niece and I love her as well, but as Tazar has said, she can hold her own, but I will be there for her if she needs us. She's very stubborn, Salas."

"Thank you," I said to both men.

Stranger things had happened to me since I had been with Kovak, but this blew my mind. The thoughts of me and Febra's passionate lovemaking still burned deep within me. But I was with Ravina, and I couldn't betray her.

EPISODE
27

I met Ravina in the garden. She was upset that her sister had betrayed the coven and Kovak, but she was enraged that she had done so with Koshen. I tried to comfort her, but she told me that it wasn't necessary.

"Salas, my sister has always been this way, selfish. It was always about her. Nothing and no one else mattered. She behaved the same way when we were humans and even after we were turned. I tried to tell her on numerous occasions that Kovak is off-limits. He was our maker. I never knew it would come to this, but what can I do?"

"There's nothing either of us can do."

"Perhaps, he'll spare her life if she surrenders."

"At least he said to take them alive."

"My sister might surrender, but I don't think Koshen will. He has his pride and he's a fierce warrior. He will fight to the death."

"I agree with you. Now that we have gotten to this point, what is it that you're supposed to tell me? Koshen asked you about it."

She took a deep breath before looking away. Turning back to me, she said, "Trajar was my lover."

"What? He was?" Words cannot describe how I felt. "Go on."

"Our coven was in a fierce battle with our enemies and Trajar was our friend during this period. We destroyed our enemies and as a gift, Kovak gave me to him. This was the practice back then in the Old World. We rewarded great deeds with whatever the victor desired. Koshen was there then, and he was angry because he desired me. He was thrilled when our friendship with Trajar ended. He was the one who spearheaded the plan for my safe return. He was there, Salas. He was the one who killed the private bodyguards that Trajar assigned me. It was then that he told me that I owed him for saving my life. Kovak in return approved of our being together and it was so. I was with him all those years until I met you. It's the truth, you can ask Kovak; he will tell you."

"There's no need for that my love, I believe you. I just wanted to know what it was that Koshen was trying to use against you."

"It never worked; I'm with you, right?"

"That I see."

"Things have taken a turn for the worse and our coven is in danger. Our survival is important to me. Other than my human father, you and Kovak have been the only men in my life; and I don't want to lose either of you. If anything should happen to our coven, I would rather spend my eternity in hell with you than return to that monster, Trajar."

"Our coven will remain, Ravina; we will not succumb to any of our enemies, and you will never be Trajar's again, never. We fight to the death. You have been a source of encouragement since I have been with you. You have kept me on my toes, and I thank you for that."

"You are welcome, my love. Kovak has a lot of admiration for you. He talks about you a lot and in the most positive ways."

"Hmm, He's a great man and warrior."

"He says you're the son, he never had."

It was humbling hearing her say this. Those words meant a lot to me. "What do you know about, Febra?"

"I haven't heard that name in quite some time. Why do you ask?"

"Isn't she Tazar's, daughter?"

"Did you ask him?"

"You tell me."

"Yes, that's his daughter, but it's a long story. It would take me days to tell you everything about her and him."

"You don't have to, Tazar told me everything."

"Why did you bring her up? Do you know her?"

"Yes, I met her a while back when I was first turned."

"Oh, Okay. But I know there's more, right?"

"Indeed, there is. She's the one who provided us with all the information."

"She did?"

"Yes. If it weren't for her, we wouldn't have known about Nalia and Koshen's plan."

KARL ANTHONY

"She must still care about her father. I wish they would rekindle their relationship. She was a great friend."

"Perhaps she will."

I had a lot on my mind that night as I slept. My body ached not from any physical work, but from all that, we had been through the last few years. I pretended at times that it wasn't happening. I would lie in bed pretending that it would all go away. I hadn't been quite as resilient as I thought I should have been, especially when it came to Koshen and Savina. Strangely, I wanted to believe that they were different and that we would all do what's best for the preservation of our coven. I was way too naive.

***

Several months had passed without any news of Koshen and Savina. We had gotten word that several of Trajar's fighters were in the surrounding area. Benjamin and I were dispatched to investigate the matter. We were traveling at a high rate of speed when we were suddenly attacked by a small group of ten male and female fighters. It was a fierce battle as we fought for our lives. I was knocked off balance as a sword whizzed by my neck, narrowly missing me. I tried to regain my footing, but I was hit by an unseen fighter. Dazed and wobbly, Benjamin yelled for me to take cover, and I did so. I couldn't believe what I saw next. It was Koshen and Savina. I pounced upon them, while Benjamin fought off the others. Within seconds, only Savina, Koshen, and one other fighter were left. He was quickly killed.

Seeing that the numbers were evenly matched, Savina bolted. I started after her but feared leaving Benjamin alone with Koshen, who was an excellent fighter. We fought bravely and valiantly. We pleaded for Koshen to surrender, but he would have none of it. He and I were exchanging blows when Benjamin yelled for me to get out of the way; luckily, I did, but unfortunately, he couldn't. The shrill, piercing sound of a flying sword found its intended target as it pierced into the back of Koshen and struck his heart. Mortally wounded, Benjamin approached him and with a scowl on his face said, "You have done a lot of evil over the years and great harm to our coven; and it's now time to meet your fate," to which Koshen with a sneer etched on his face, screamed, he would see us all in hell. Turning our backs, we began walking away, as the wind blew his remains in the evening dusk.

***

Benjamin and I entered the mansion disheveled and unsettled. We quickly made our way to Kovak's private library as the others looked on. They could tell we had been in a fight. A lot of questions were being asked. But I explained to them that I had to talk to Kovak. He was having a drink when we entered.

"What brings you here in such a rush?"

"It's about Koshen and Savina," I said, handing him Koshen's sword. He paused momentarily. "We fought with them and Koshen is dead. Savina got away."

"Hmm," he grimaced, "this is the sword that I gave him many years ago."

"I thought you would want it returned."

"Thank you for returning it. So, he wouldn't surrender?"

"No, we pleaded with him, but he wouldn't. We were on routine patrol like you ordered when we were ambushed by at least ten of their fighters. It was a vicious fight, but he just wouldn't surrender."

"He chose his destiny. He betrayed my trust. As for Savina, did she fight?"

"She fought in small bursts. It was unorthodox. I had never seen anyone fight like that before."

"She's a warrior! She's been fighting that way for as long as I can recall. Benjamin, I have said this to you before, I'm deeply sorry for your loss. We all have lost someone during this ordeal."

"Thank you, Kovak, I'm humbled," he replied.

"We must continue the patrol until she's captured. We must remain relentless. Tell the others what I said. I will tell them about Koshen. Leave me now."

Despite Koshen's betrayal, I felt Kovak's pain. Koshen was like a son and losing him had to hurt. When you have groomed someone all those years and then things take a turn for the worse, it's a pain, not even time can heal. I understood that much. Someone must have told Ravina that I had returned. She was waiting for me as I walked into the living quarters. I greeted her.

"What happened?" she asked.

"Koshen is dead . . ."

"And my sister?"

"She got away. They attacked us. We never saw them."

"Who was with you?"

"Benjamin."

"I see. How did she look?"

"She looked the same. But I can't believe she attacked us. They were lying in wait for us."

"I wish she would surrender and ask Kovak's forgiveness. Was it you who killed, Koshen?"

"Benjamin did. I returned his sword."

"I sense a bad omen. My mind is troubled, and I fear that Trajar's intent this time is the total annihilation of our coven. I'm deeply worried."

"I am too, but we are prepared to battle."

"Give me a moment, I will return."

"Where are you going?"

"To see Kovak, I need to have a word with him."

"About?"

"Savina."

"Go ahead. I'll be in the garden." I was worried about her.

EPISODE
28

"Kovak, what if I were to find Savina and bring her to you?" Ravina asked.

"I will not allow that. What purpose would that serve?"

"I'm pleading for her life. Keep her in isolation, anything, and all I'm asking is that you spare her life."

"What she has done says a lot about her character. She jeopardizes our lives, yours included, because of her selfish ways. It was her decision. It was her choice."

"I'm begging you. Please, Kovak, she's all I've got." She was hoping that he would reconsider.

"If she's captured alive, I will grant your wish. But I do not want you out on patrol."

"I promise. I won't!"

As I listened to her, I wanted to know if she would keep her word; to which she said she would. That night, she, and I, along with Benjamin and Isabel decided to go into town. Unlike the town's people who were drinking beer and other strong alcoholic beverages and acting rowdy, we drank from the last supply of blood from the second battle of the Civil War. We had amassed a considerable supply that would last us for an extended period. We discussed what would become of us if we were taken prisoners by Trajar.

"I can't foresee that," I said to them.

"I'll fight to the death," Benjamin said.

"And I'll fight alongside you," Isabel added.

"I admire the lot of you, for your bravery," Ravina smiled at us. Pointing towards the waters, she said aloud how she wished she could return to the Old Country.

"Is it as beautiful as they say?" Isabel asked.

"Yes, it is! Oh, how I miss the times Savina, and I would spend at our parent's old hut, playing without a care in the world . . ."

"So why did you come to the New World?"

"Kovak brought us here."

"And you have been here ever since?"

"No, I visited a few times. The last was about nine hundred years ago."

"My, that is a long time," Isabel stated.

"Yes, and I long for it."

It wasn't long before our conversation ended. The drunken townspeople and sea merchants had become boisterous and unruly. A large battalion of police had been called to disperse the unruly crowd. Not wanting to be singled out, we returned to the mansion.

***

The Death-knell had sounded. Trajar had arrived and settled in Connecticut. He was prepared for an all-out battle. He had the manpower and felt invincible. We were told by our spies, that in his company was a vampire, no one had seen before. He was called, Landar. Physically, he was much older than both Kovak and Tazar, which meant that he was turned at an older age. But he wasn't an old vampire in terms of years. They said he was accompanied by a beautiful woman, who wasn't of the same persuasion as he. We could care less about who accompanied him from the Old World. What mattered to us was our survival and nothing else.

Our coven was on high alert as we awaited Trajar's next move. A sharp-thinking Kovak devised a cunning plan. Trajar was welcome with open arms by his allies, including fighters from the Xeras coven. They planned a huge celebration for him. It was the talk of vampiredom. I guess Trajar and his minions outsmarted themselves by not keeping it within their circle. Kovak chose me, Benjamin, and Isabel to infiltrate their festivities and to gather whatever information we could. I convinced Kovak to permit me to ask Febra along; he did.

I met with her two days before the celebration at Trajar's mansion in Connecticut. Ravina was made aware of what we were about to do. She was worried about me, but I assured her that I would be fine. That very same day, I brought Febra with me to the mansion. Our members hissed and snarled upon seeing her. Not one to shy away from a squabble or attention, she returned their hisses and snarls. I told my brothers and sisters to remain calm because she was an ally, not an enemy.

I escorted her to her father's library, where we met Kovak. It was an awkward moment, to say the least, as the two refused to say much to each other. She greeted Kovak, who insisted that she speak to her father. We left them alone for some time. Upon our return, the tension had eased some and they were talking. What they discuss? I had no idea. I was relieved. The look on Kovak's face told the same story.

"Come," Kovak said. We were taken to the Argi. Benjamin and Isabel had never been up close with the Argi before; rarely did the others see them.

"What is this?" Benjamin whispered to me.

"I don't know, but I wouldn't worry about it."

"Okay."

"Here, take this," one of the Argi said, handing us each several small tubes filled with blood. None of us questioned it, apart from Febra, and rightfully so.

"This is to keep your scent hidden from our enemies, especially that tyrant, Trajar," the Argi responded. We took it as told.

"Come now," Kovak insisted. "Let us bid you farewell. You must be amongst the revelers from this point on and not at the last second. I chose you three because Trajar isn't familiar with any of you. As for you Febra, it's been a long time since he's laid eyes on you. But at the same time, be mindful of the Xeras. Do you wish to say anything?"

KARL ANTHONY

"Father," Febra said aloud, "your sworn enemies are mine as well. Uncle, your sworn enemies are mine also. Mother, your sworn enemies are mine. We fight for the Vladzann coven. We fight for the Dalical coven." We joined in as Kovak, Tazar, Ravina and the Argi looked on. In a blur, we were gone.

***

Time was on our side as we mingled and chatted with those we came in contact with, in the small town of Bantam. A handful of them spoke with foreign accents. Whatever was in the blood-filled tube that we drank, it worked. We easily figured out our enemies from amongst the townspeople. It seemed as if Trajar had brought half of the Old World with him.

I must say, it was a grand sight, seeing the grandeur and brilliance of what awaited us. I was nervous as were the others, except for Febra. She was fearless. All she talked about was ripping Trajar apart. I had to remind her that wasn't our mission. And that we should follow the plan through.

On the day of the celebration, we were ushered to the main house. It was a rambunctious crowd. They were noisy, youthful, out of control, and energetic. There was an elderly crowd, which displayed an air of nobility and slight arrogance with the youthful energy of the younger crowd.

We immediately began focusing our attention on the group. But Trajar and his hierarchy hadn't arrived yet, and so we waited. Moments later, the music abruptly stopped. The dancing, laughter, and talking came to an immediate halt. Then without warning, it started once again, only this time, there was a huge procession of men and women, lined on both sides of the sprawling room. The decorative chandeliers adorned with candles lit up the room. Luckily, upon our arrival in Bantam, we were told that it was an all-black affair.

It was an Old-World display of great splendor and magnificence pomp as Trajar entered the Ballroom with not only a stunning raven-haired beauty; she was young-looking. Following closely behind was an elderly gentleman along with a copper-skinned beauty. She looked quite young herself. I assumed the elderly gentleman was, Landar. He was some distance from me; thus, I couldn't get a clear look. We were told to position ourselves somewhere between the middle and the back of the room. We stood in the back.

Trajar gestured with his hand and the music stopped. He smiled at his followers and began talking. "We have come from the Great Country to take what is rightfully ours. The blood of our makers and our brothers and sisters were not shed in vain, and we will not stay put and allow our nemesis to desecrate our legacy. We are the RICA. WE ARE THE DOMINANT RULER."

There was a thunderous roar as they began chanting the very words. We stared at each other. The fervor had reached epic proportions, it made us nervous. But we were resolute and intended to remain so, as Trajar continued. "Our sworn enemies, Kovak and Tazar will soon feel the wrath of our power, along with their allies. We will send them to their eternity and all of vampiredom will know that we are RICA, THE DOMINANT RULER. In two days, we will march on Kovak and his coven. Once he's annihilated, we will crush the others easily."

KARL ANTHONY

There was a thunderous outburst. We tried not to show our anger as a small group standing next to us, kept repeating how much of a wonderful leader Trajar is and that he will crush his enemies. I tugged on Febra to remain calm. She smiled at me. I couldn't help but laugh to myself.

"My children," Trajar continued. "I welcome amongst you, Landar and his beautiful beloved, Danar."

They turned and faced the crowd. Suddenly, my entire world ended. My knees buckled. My mind was reeling back and forth. I had to get away. The others saw the look on my face.

"Is that who I think it is?" Benjamin and Isabel asked, shocked.

"Let's go," I said.

"Why? What happened?" Febra asked.

"Come, let's go," I commanded them.

"How dare you walked out on our leader?" several men standing in the back said to us.

"Fuck, you!" Febra yelled at them, before snapping the neck of the man standing closest to her. We left in a flash. They were on our tail when they suddenly turned around. We continued before taking a rest.

"Febra, why?" I said to her.

"Fuck them, and remember this, you are not my maker."

"We could have been killed."

"Yes, but did we?"

"Okay, Febra."

"What was that all about?" she asked me, wanting an answer. I told her who it was and my reasons for leaving.

"I'm sorry, Salas," she said.

"Thanks."

"Salas, he resembles, Buchanan! It's him, isn't it?" Benjamin questioned.

"Yes!"

"I used to hate it when he would visit our home."

"I did also," Isabel added.

"Fuck, and that was, Evelyn?"

"Indeed, it is Benjamin," I answered.

"How did he become friends with Trajar and ended up in the Old World?"

"I really can't answer that now, Benjamin."

"Are you okay, Salas?" Isabel asked.

"Yes, I am. Come, let's go home."

EPILOGUE

We informed Kovak and Tazar of Trajar's plan. They quickly warned the coven and preparation were made for battle. Febra was asked if her coven was willing to fight alongside us. She said she would have an answer for us the next day. Within two days, Trajar and his army would be upon us, Kovak and Tazar reminded her. She said not to worry because she was confident that her mother's coven would not let an opportunity like this pass them by. I was confident that they would join us.

I hadn't shared with Kovak and Tazar that I was convinced that Landar was Buchanan. I sat down with them.

"It was him," I said to them. Benjamin and Isabel backed up what I said.

"And you're saying that the young woman he's with is, Evelyn?"

"Yes."

"It's possible that Trajar showed up after we left. Evelyn was hurt by then, and Buchanan was still alive, although he had lost his mind. If that's the case, then it would make sense that he turned them both and took them back to the Old country."

"It does make sense."

"They had to change Evelyn's thought process because Buchanan treated you and her harshly. Once this was done, Trajar gave her to that bastard."

"What do I do now, Kovak?"

"For starters my son, you have a choice."

"What do you mean?"

"She doesn't know that you exist. You can keep it that way, or you can make yourself known. But then, you have to ask yourself this question."

"And what's that?"

"Where does Ravina fits in all this? These are some of the things that you must take into consideration. Have you told her?"

"No, I haven't. I will once I'm done here."

"My son, I can only imagine how you feel. But we must remain aggressive and vigilant in our quest to defeat Trajar."

"Indeed. I'm ready. Now, if you'll excuse me, I will go and see her."

"Certainly!"

***

KARL ANTHONY

I didn't know where to begin as I sat down with her. She saw the troubled look on my face.

"What is wrong?" she asked.

"I saw someone from my past at Trajar's place."

"What do you mean someone from your past? Who is it?"

"Evelyn!" She couldn't believe what she was hearing.

"How could that be? I thought she couldn't be saved that night."

"It's obvious that Trajar paid the Big House a visit after Kovak left her."

"I'm so sorry. I don't know what else to say."

"There's not much that you can say."

"Trajar has always been evil. Was she alone or was she with someone?"

"She was with Landar, he and Buchanan are one and the same."

"Oh, no! Trajar turned him too?"

"Yes. I don't know what to do."

"The Old Country is where some of the most powerful vampires are. They will kill as freely as the wind blows. No remorse. Their chain of command is solid and must be followed. They have trained both of them well."

"You are right, but what do I do now? What?"

"I don't know. But whatever you choose to do, I'll support you."

"Thank you, it means a lot to me."

The next day, Febra arrived with the good news that her coven would fight with us. She wanted to know if Ravina was my beloved. I said, yes. I could tell she wasn't thrilled. They were friends from the Old country, and I understood.

***

The fall of 1882 was significant for our coven. After years of threats, the time had come for us to fight or be annihilated. Trajar and his goons launched an assault on us at a place called Wilderness on the outskirt of a desolate town. On that cool morning, nine hundred fighters accompanied us into battle against Trajar and his army of twelve hundred.

Trajar sent a small army of about two hundred to launch an assault. We fought for our lives as we had them on their heels. We had a small number of casualties as we prepared for another attack. Seeing that his small number of fighters couldn't withstand our attack, he attacked us with another army of fighters. Kovak took advantage of his miscalculation by simultaneously attacking him from the rear, left, and right sides. As they tried to escape, they had no other options other than to fight to the death. We slaughtered them. We fought non-stop for the next two hours. We pulled them from the trees and those who tried to scale the walls and huge boulders that bordered the area were executed.

With most of his fighters wounded or dead, Trajar, his beloved, Landar, and Danar along with members of his hierarchy made a bid to escape, but it wasn't to be. I was in a vicious fight with members of his rank and file when I was hit from behind. It was a powerful blow. I looked up. I froze. It was her. She had a stunned look on her face.

"John? Is it you?" she asked, unsure.

"Yes, it's me, Evelyn."

"But . . ."

"I thought the same thing. Come." I took her to an area away from the fighting. "Who is your maker?"

"That night," she began. "I was dying after getting bit. To this day, I can't recall who it was. What I do know, is that I was laying on the floor dying, when I noticed Trajar standing over me. Moments later, I felt a searing pain in my neck. It was he, who turned me and Buchanan. I was then taken to the Old World along with a few others. I was held captive all these years because I refused to take Buchanan as my lover. I was violated by Trajar, but he wouldn't allow Buchanan to do the same. All those years, I wondered what became of you and the children. I had given up hope. It was only when Trajar returned to the Old World and informed us that we would return with him, did I go along with it. I thought I had lost you forever."

Suddenly, I heard a loud hiss, and the blade of a sword missed me by inches. It was Savina. I hadn't expected her. She wasn't on the battlefield. I was caught off guard. There were another loud hiss and a snap. I turned to see Evelyn with the head of one of Trajar's fighters in her hand. I was trapped by Buchanan and two others.

"Danar, what have you done?" Buchanan screamed at her. She didn't respond. "And who is this, Savina?"

"It's me, you bastard!" I yelled at him. "You killed my children."

"What the fuck! John is that you?" Realizing that it was me, he smiled and said, "I knew I would see you again. I knew they had made you one of the undead. But today, you will meet your maker along with that whore. I want you to know this, John. You both belong to me. Do you hear me? You belong to me! He laughed. Funny, she never loved me, John. She loved you! She would always talk about her dearest fucking, John. So yes, I'm going to fucking kill both of you."

I pounced upon him before he could defend himself. Evelyn and I ripped him apart and tore the heads from the other's body. Seeing this, Savina took off. I took after her, but I lost her scent. I was in a daze. Evelyn had found her way back into my life and I almost lost her again.

We made our way back to the battlefield. There in chains were Trajar, his beloved Queen, and eighty of his fighters. Kovak immediately noticed Evelyn. Our fighters hissed and snarled at her. Kovak immediately told them that she was a friend, and they quiet down. The prisoners were then taken to the mansion, where they were quickly executed in the dungeon. With only him and his Queen remaining, and facing his eternal death, an unremorseful Trajar remained stoic, as he awaited his fate with his maker.

"Where is Nalia?" Kovak asked. "Fetch her." She was made aware of Kovak's request and hurried there.

"Come here," he said. She stood in front of him and Trajar. "Do you know her?" he said to Trajar.

He studied her face and then said, "No."

"Bring me my sword." Kovak placed the blade on the neck of Trajar's, Queen, and asked him once again, "Do you know her? If you lie to me, I will send your beloved to her maker."

"Yes, I know her," he said, dejectedly.

"Are you her maker, or was it someone else from your coven? Answer me? Were you the one who turned, Danar?"

"It was I who turned Danar, but it was Tasia who turned the young, Nalia. Tasia left her amongst us never to return."

"And why is that?"

"She was destroyed by one of your covens in the Old Country."

"Tasia wasn't any good. Like you, she should have met her maker a long time ago."

"I have told you all that you asked. Now, can you spare my beloved?"

Kovak turned and looked at Tazar and then at us, and then slowly began saying, "Aptissimus Quisque Tantum Superest, Numai Cel Mai Tare Supravietuieste."

The pitch increased and reverberated throughout the dungeon as we repeated our coven's mantra. Febra looked at me and then at her father, as she repeated the words. I was surprised, but then it dawned on me that she was a part of two covens. I smiled at her, and she reciprocated.

Kovak then held his sword above his head and brought it down on the neck of Trajar's, Queen. Trajar yelled out a loud and painful hiss as our roar continued.

"Kovak, Tazar, I will see you both in hell. Others will come after you that I can assure you. Fuck, you!"

Kovak wielded the sword once again and brought it down on his neck. The once-mighty Trajar, the vampire who had a reputation as a maverick was nothing more than dust in the wind.

***

"Who was Tasia?" I asked Kovak, moments later.

"She was close to Ravina and Savina once upon a time. Sort of an older sister, but she betrayed a few covens in the Old Country, and I forbid her from socializing with ours."

"Was she of our coven?"

"No."

"It all makes sense now. Nalia carried the scent of Tasia's coven."

"Ahh, my son, doesn't it?"

Kovak explained a lot to me that night. I was satisfied and more than relieved that Trajar was no longer in our midst. I excused myself and sat down with Ravina. I told her that Evelyn and I fought with Savina, but that she got away. The look in her eyes pained my heart because she feared for her sister.

I was hoping for the best, but things don't always work out as planned. Ravina was not happy to see, Evelyn. She was upset that both Evelyn and Febra were now amongst us. I wasn't interested in Febra, and Kovak assured her of that. Evelyn was another matter; I didn't know what to do. My hands were tied. Ravina thought that I would run off with her, which wasn't the case. But I understood her feelings.

I brought all this to Kovak's attention. Not only was he an astute leader, but his judgment and decision-making skills were also based on reason and logic, and he came up with a solution. He had Evelyn stay with the Zemcan coven, one of our closest allies. I would visit her, but she was forbidden to visit our coven without Kovak's approval. At times, we related well, and at other times it was very awkward. She wanted to know if Ravina and I were lovers. I told her that we were. She did not react. She smiled and said that she understood.

KARL ANTHONY

I was in mourning for months. The death of my children resonated deeply within me. I would never see them again. I pleaded in private with Kovak and Tazar that I no longer wanted to remain with the coven. They were worried about me. They convinced me that I needed some closure and that at least my children weren't one of the undead. In some ways, it did ease the pain.

One year later . . .

We were getting death threats from some of the scattered covens who were still loyal to Trajar. We were prepared, because it was only a year earlier that we rid vampiredom of the evil, Trajar. That said, Kovak and Tazar decided to visit the Old Country. An invitation was sent by the Old-World Council of Vampires, requesting their presence.

I was put in charge until their return. The Argi and the Council were there to see to it that I followed procedures. We bid them farewell. I longed to see the Old World. Kovak promised that I would accompany him on his next trip. They were gone for a month when we received word from Febra's coven that they were kidnapped by fighters, loyal to Trajar. My first reaction was how to tell Isabel, but after discussing it with the Council and the Argi, I decided not to.

I had made up my mind to visit the Old World, and the Council and the Argi agreed. I decided to take Benjamin, Febra, Ravina, and Evelyn with me. We were going to bring our King home. But I reminded them that Savina was still alive and well.

I had a lot on my mind as I lay next to Ravina that night. The thoughts of Evelyn and the events leading up to the capture of Kovak troubled me; I contemplated for some time whether it made sense to bring both Ravina and Evelyn with me to the Old World.

Ravina must have sensed my restlessness. She put her arms around me and held me close upon hearing my decision. She stared into my eyes. She meant the world to me. But my heart was now conflicted, as I wondered about, Evelyn.

My life with Ravina was unlike anything that I had lived before. Maybe it's because I am one of the undead, but to put it bluntly, she made me appreciate everything negative that the humans say about us, and how our vampire enemies now look upon us. I am now free to take off the cloak of feeling sorry for myself and truly become the leader that I am because I am Aptissimus Quisque Tantum Superest, Numai Cel Mai Tare Supravietuieste.